The Wedding Day Mystery

Patti took a deep breath, then opened the box. Mandy, Nancy, George, and Bess peeked in.

Inside was a bride-and-groom cake ornament—or what remained of it. The heads of the figurines had been broken off.

"I don't get it," Bess murmured, puzzled. "What is this—some sick joke?"

Next to the ornament was a piece of paper. Nancy reached in and pulled it out.

Written on it in large bold letters were the words:

YOUR WEDING IS DOOMED
STOP IT BEFORE ITS TOO LATE

Nancy Drew
Mystery Stories

Available from MINSTREL Books

NANCY DREW® 136

THE WEDDING DAY MYSTERY

CAROLYN KEENE

A MINSTREL® BOOK

Published by POCKET BOOKS
New York   London   Toronto   Sydney   Tokyo   Singapore

This book is a work of fiction. Names, characters, places and incidents are products of the author's imagination or are used fictitiously. Any resemblance to actual events or locales or persons living or dead is entirely coincidental.

A MINSTREL PAPERBACK *Original*

 A Minstrel Book published by
POCKET BOOKS, a division of Simon & Schuster Inc.
1230 Avenue of the Americas, New York, NY 10020

Copyright © 1997 by Simon & Schuster Inc.
Produced by Mega-Books, Inc.

ISBN: 0-671-00050-0

First Minstrel Books printing April 1997

10 9 8 7 6 5 4 3 2 1

NANCY DREW, NANCY DREW MYSTERY STORIES,
A MINSTREL BOOK and colophon are registered
trademarks of Simon & Schuster Inc.

Cover art by Ernie Norcia

Printed in the U.S.A.

Contents

THE WEDDING DAY MYSTERY

1

A Weekend of Weddings

Bess Marvin draped an antique lace veil over her long blond hair and checked her reflection in the rearview mirror. "What do you think?" she asked brightly. "Don't I make a cool bride?"

Bess, her cousin George Fayne, and their friend Nancy Drew were on their way to a wedding. George, who was sitting in the passenger seat, turned around to glance at Bess. "Very pretty," she said. "But that veil doesn't exactly go with your purple dress."

Eighteen-year-old Nancy, behind the wheel of her blue Mustang, peered in the rearview mirror and chuckled. "I think George is right. You need either an antique lace dress or a purple veil."

"A purple veil—what a great idea!" Bess exclaimed. She reached up to remove the veil, but

1

it was caught on one of her earrings. "Hey, what's with this thing?" she muttered, tugging at the lace.

"Be careful, Bess," George warned. "If anything happens to that veil, Mandy will kill you and so will the bride!"

Mandy Applebaum was Bess's boss and the owner of a wedding consulting service called Happily Ever After, Inc. Mandy arranged weddings, taking care of all the details including the setting, attire, invitations, food, photography, music, and flowers.

This weekend Mandy was in charge of four weddings. They were all taking place at Heights House, a Victorian mansion on the outskirts of River Heights. Because Mandy was so busy, Bess had suggested that she hire Nancy and George as extra helpers. Mandy had agreed, so Bess, Nancy, and George were on their way to assist with the first wedding of the weekend.

Bess finally untangled the delicate veil and put it back in its tissue-filled box. The veil had been at the dressmaker's undergoing minor repairs, and Mandy had asked her to pick it up on the way to the wedding. "There, good as new," Bess announced, rearranging her hair. She pointed out the window and said, "Oh, there's the turnoff for Heights House, Nan."

Nancy flicked on her turn signal and swung onto the narrow dirt road. Alongside the road were masses of lilac bushes in bloom and rolling meadows that looked golden in the late-afternoon light. A half dozen old farmhouses dotted the landscape. Gazing at the rural scenery, Nancy couldn't believe they were only fifteen minutes from downtown River Heights.

"Wait till you guys see Heights House," Bess said eagerly. "It's gorgeous. There are huge chandeliers everywhere, and there's the most amazing ballroom."

"That's where tonight's reception will be held, right?" George spoke up.

"Right," Bess replied. "And tomorrow night's reception, too. But the other two receptions will be outdoors." She sighed and shook her head. "This weekend is going to be exhausting. I've been working part-time for Mandy since April, and we've never had four back-to-back weddings."

"It *is* June, after all," Nancy reminded her. "June is traditionally the most popular month for weddings."

"I think it'll be fun having a marathon work weekend," George said cheerfully, "even though I had to pass up a chance to run in a *real* marathon on Sunday."

"A marathon—as in running twenty-six point something miles? Of your own free will?" Bess shuddered. "No, thank you!"

Nancy couldn't help smiling. Even though

George and Bess were cousins, they were as different as night and day. Not only were they opposites physically—George was a tall, slender brunette with brown eyes, while Bess was short, blond, and blue-eyed—but they were opposites in personality, too. George's idea of a good time was mountain climbing or camping in the wilderness. Bess preferred shopping or reading fashion magazines.

"So, speaking of work, what kind of stuff will we be doing for Mandy tonight?" George asked Bess.

"Oh, a little of everything," Bess said. "Helping the bride and her attendants get ready, putting centerpieces on the tables, chopping vegetables for the caterer, serving hors d'oeuvres—you name it." She grinned and added, "It's a zoo, but you get used to it pretty fast. And you'll like working for Mandy, even though she's kind of serious."

Five minutes later Nancy pulled into the winding driveway of Heights House, which was several hundred yards from its nearest neighbor. Bess was right. The place *was* gorgeous. It was an enormous stone mansion with wide front steps, stained-glass windows, arches, and several cylindrical towers with candle-snuffer caps. It reminded Nancy of a medieval castle.

"There are pretty garden paths out back, and a duck pond and a huge forest, too," Bess said.

"There's also a big gazebo. That's where wedding number two is going to be held." She paused and frowned. "Or is it wedding number four?"

After Nancy parked the car in the lot, they went into the house. The inside was as grand as the outside. There was a wrought-iron chandelier in the large front hall and a stone staircase curving up to the second floor. Hanging on the wall of the entrance hall were portraits of a gray-haired man with wire-rimmed glasses and a white-haired woman with pale blue eyes. Following Nancy's gaze, Bess said, "That's Joseph and Jeanine Merrill. They were the original owners of the house."

Just then a tall, slim woman in a beige linen pantsuit came rushing down the stairs, clipboard in hand. She appeared to be in her early thirties and had short brown hair and large brown eyes.

The woman didn't notice Nancy, George, and Bess until she was at the bottom of the stairs. She stopped and glanced at them with a startled expression. "Oh, great, you're here," she said quickly. "And, Bess, I see you brought the veil with you." She turned to Nancy and George and stuck her hand out. "You must be Nancy Drew and George Fayne. I'm Mandy Applebaum."

"I'm Nancy and this is George," Nancy said, shaking Mandy's hand. "How are things going?"

"The florist shorted us one bouquet and I can't

get him on the phone," Mandy said breathlessly. "So we have to dismantle the other bouquets and create an extra one. Plus, the bride and her attendants need help getting ready. Oh, and we have to put about a hundred candles in the chapel."

"Why so many?" George asked her.

"This is going to be a Victorian-style wedding, with authentic details," Mandy explained. "That means a candlelight ceremony, Victorian attire, Victorian menu, you name it."

"It sounds so romantic," Bess said with a sigh.

"It sounds like there's a lot to do," Nancy said to Mandy. "Where do you want us to start?"

"Why don't I introduce you to the bride and her attendants first?" Mandy said. "We'll see what they need from us, then we can tackle the other problems."

The four of them headed upstairs, where Mandy knocked on a closed door. "This is the Gold Room," she told them. "It's where all the brides get dressed." She raised her voice and called out, "Libby? It's me, Mandy."

"Mandy, help!" a voice rang out.

Mandy frowned, then opened the door and rushed in. Nancy and her friends followed. Two women in their late twenties—a redhead and a blond—were sitting on a gold brocade settee. The redhead was wearing a floor-length, pale pink dress. The blond was wearing an old-fashioned ivory-colored wedding gown made of muslin and lace. The room was furnished with beautiful antiques, and the walls, drapes, and rugs were all shades of yellow and gold.

Seeing Mandy, the woman in the wedding gown jumped up and ran to her. "Look at this!" she shrieked, pointing to a scarlet smear on the front of her dress. "Lipstick! I managed to get *lipstick* on my great-grandmother's wedding dress while I was putting it on. What am I going to do?"

Mandy put her hand on the woman's shoulder. "Don't worry about it, Libby," she said soothingly. "I've got a special wedding emergency kit downstairs, and there's something in there for lipstick stains."

Libby's face lit up. "Really?"

"Really. Club soda and talcum powder— works every time. I'll go down and get them right now." She waved her clipboard at Nancy and her friends and said, "These are my assistants, Nancy Drew, Bess Marvin, and George Fayne. And this is the bride, Libby Ewing, and her maid of honor, Molly Croog." She glanced around the room. "Where are the bridesmaids?"

"They went to get some sodas," Molly replied. "Hey, did you manage to find a bouquet for Emily Sherman?"

"Don't worry, that's being taken care of," Mandy said easily.

7

Watching Mandy in action, Nancy was amazed. Gone was the frantic, stressed-out person she'd met in the front hall. With Libby and Molly, the wedding consultant was calm, cool, and reassuring—completely on top of things.

The door opened a crack, and a petite brunette popped her head in. "Um, Lib? Can I talk to you for a sec?"

"What is it, Emily?" Libby sat down at the dressing table and sniffed delicately at a vase of long-stemmed yellow roses. Then she began fixing her lipstick.

Emily walked in, stood awkwardly in the middle of the room, and glanced uncomfortably at everyone. "It's Charles," she said slowly. "He seems to be, um, missing."

Bess leaned toward Nancy and George and whispered, "Charles is the groom."

Libby whirled around. The color had drained from her face. "Missing? What do you mean, he's missing?" she rasped.

"The best man—what's his name, Tyler—just called," Emily explained uneasily. "He was supposed to go by Charles's apartment to pick him up. But he said that when he got there, no one answered the bell, and the door was locked. He went to a phone booth and called Charles's number, but all he got was the answering machine."

8

"I'm sure it's just a mix-up," Mandy said quickly. "I'm sure that Charles is—"

"—standing me up!" Libby finished. Hiding her face in her hands, she burst into tears. "I'm being . . . stood up on . . . my wedding day," she sputtered.

Molly put her arm around Libby's shoulders. "Listen, Lib—"

"No, I will *not* listen!" Libby wailed. "Leave me alone, all of you. I want to be left alone." She picked up the vase of yellow roses, aimed it at the wall, and threw it. There was a loud crash, and crystal shards and rose petals flew everywhere.

Seeing that Libby was dead serious, Nancy, George, Bess, Mandy, Molly, and Emily hurried out of the room. The door slammed behind them, and Nancy heard the sound of the lock being turned.

"She's not usually like this," Molly said apologetically to the others. "It's just that she's really on edge about this wedding. She and Charles have been dating for about seven years, and they're finally getting married. Libby wants everything to be absolutely perfect."

"I understand," Mandy said sympathetically. "Molly, Emily, why don't the three of us go downstairs and get on the phone? Maybe we can track Charles down." She turned to Nancy, George, and Bess. "You can work on the bouquet.

Bess, you know how, right? All the flowers are in the Blue Room."

"No problem," Bess said. Nancy and George nodded.

Nancy, George, and Bess went down the hall to the Blue Room. Inside, they were greeted by a blast of air conditioning and the overwhelming fragrance of flowers. The floor was covered with boxes and vases filled with white roses, jasmine, and orange blossoms.

Bess picked up a spool of wire and some wire cutters from the dresser, then pointed to three small bouquets nestled in a large white box. "Let's each take one and pull it apart."

They got to work. "I feel so bad for Libby," Nancy said. "First the florist shorts her one bouquet, then she gets lipstick on her wedding dress, and now she can't find her fiancé."

Bess pulled a strand of orange blossoms out of one of the bouquets. "She seemed so upset," she murmured. "Maybe one of us should go down the hall and check on her. Or maybe—"

She was interrupted by a loud, shrill scream.

2

A Ghostly Visitor

"That sounded like Libby!" Nancy cried. She jumped to her feet and ran out the door. George and Bess followed. Another scream rang out, louder this time. It was definitely coming from Libby's dressing room.

Nancy got to Libby's door and jiggled the knob. It was still locked. "Libby," she shouted, "open up! It's me, Nancy Drew!"

There was no reply. "Do you think she's hurt?" Bess whispered nervously.

"I don't know," Nancy said. "Why don't you find Mandy and see if she's got a key? No, wait a second, this will be faster." She reached into her purse, which was slung across her shoulder, and got out a credit card. Then she began picking at the lock.

After a moment, Nancy had the lock undone, and she, George, and Bess burst into the room.

Libby was standing in front of the closet door, staring at it with a horrified expression. She looked as though she was in shock.

Nancy rushed up to her and touched her arm. "Libby?" she said gently. "Libby, are you all right? We heard you screaming."

"A—a ghost," Libby stammered. She pointed a trembling finger at the closet door. "I—I just saw a ghost in there. It had a skeleton head, and it was wearing a long black velvet cape."

Bess gasped. "You're kidding! A ghost? Do you think it's still in there?"

Nancy and George exchanged a quick, troubled glance. Nancy wondered if Libby was seeing things, possibly because of her heightened emotional state. Or maybe someone had played a prank on her.

Nancy went up to the closet door and pressed her ear against it. No noise was coming from the other side. Tentatively, she opened the door.

"What are you doing?" Libby asked nervously, backing up. "Didn't you hear what I said? There's a ghost in there!"

Nancy peered into the closet. "There's no one in here, Libby. A couple of dresses, but otherwise it's empty."

Pushing the dresses aside, Nancy stepped inside the closet and looked around. It was lined with cedar panels. It also appeared to have been cleaned recently; there was no dust anywhere.

Frowning, Nancy ran her fingers over the panels. Then she began tapping on them lightly with her fingertips. There was one dull thud after another until she reached a panel near the back of the closet. It made a hollow-sounding noise.

"Bingo," Nancy said, excited. She knelt down on the floor and ran her hands across the panel, trying to slide it in one direction or another. It didn't budge. Then she pushed against it, hard. It came loose.

Nancy pushed the panel all the way through the opening. On the other side was a dark passageway.

"Yes!" Nancy whispered. She reached into her purse and took out a small flashlight, which she always carried with her. Flicking it on, she pointed it through the opening. The passageway was just big enough for a person to crawl through.

"I found a secret passageway," Nancy called out to the others. "I'm going to check it out. You guys stay put, okay?"

Bess popped her head into the closet. "Be careful, Nan. That ghost could be dangerous."

"I'll be careful, Bess." Nancy smiled at her.

Pushing her reddish blond hair over her shoulders, Nancy got down on her hands and knees and crawled through the small opening. The passageway went on for about ten feet, then abruptly turned to the right. She came across no footprints or other clues.

She finally reached a space where she was able to stand up. After walking down one long corridor and then another, she found herself at the head of a narrow, creaky-looking set of stairs. Stepping carefully, she started down the flight. Eventually, the stairs dead-ended at a wall.

There's got to be a way through! Nancy thought in frustration. She pointed her flashlight at the wall and studied every inch of it but found nothing. She was about to give up when she noticed that one section of the wall didn't seem quite even with the rest of it.

She pushed against the odd section. It swung open silently, and the dark passageway was flooded with light. Nancy blinked. Before her was a room lined floor to ceiling with books and furnished with big leather chairs and oak tables. It appeared that she had stumbled upon the mansion's library.

It also appeared that she wasn't alone. Across the room a man was standing with his back to her. He had short dark hair and he was wearing a black tuxedo. He was humming to himself, turning something over in his hands.

Nancy stepped quietly into the room and shut the wall—which was a bookshelf on the other side—behind her. The man didn't turn around.

"Excuse me," Nancy said.

The man whirled around. He was hardly a man at all, more like a teenager. He was holding a small Chinese vase. "W—who are you?" he stammered. "And where did you come from?"

Nancy didn't reply. She wondered who he was. She also wondered what he was doing with the Chinese vase, which looked expensive. Was he a thief?

Nancy walked across the library toward him. "Nice vase," she remarked casually. "Ming dynasty, isn't it?"

"Yes, well, I was just admiring it myself," the young man muttered. He set the vase down on a nearby table, then fixed his nervous-looking green eyes on Nancy. "Anyway, as I was saying, who *are* you?"

"Nancy Drew," she said. "And you are?"

"Freddy Ewing," he replied.

"Ewing," Nancy repeated. "That must mean you're—"

"A relative of the bride," Freddy cut in. "I'm Libby's cousin. You've probably never heard of me, though. I'm from the poor branch of the Ewings, and they don't like to talk about us much." He sounded bitter.

"What are you doing in here?" Nancy asked him.

"Waiting for the circus to start, what do you think?" Freddy stared at Nancy's denim skirt and pink shirt curiously. "What about you? Didn't you read the invitation? Formal dress was requested, preferably Victorian."

"I work for Mandy Applebaum, the wedding consultant," Nancy explained.

"Oh." Freddy reached up to fix his tie, then started for the door. "Well, it's been fun chatting with you, but I think I'll go outside now and get some fresh air."

Nancy put her hand on his arm, stopping him. "Why are you here so early? The wedding isn't due to start for another hour."

"I wasn't aware that the hired help was supposed to interrogate the guests," Freddy said coldly. "Excuse me." He brushed her hand off and sauntered out the door.

Nancy stared after him curiously. What was his story? Could he have been the ghost Libby saw in her closet? Was it only a coincidence that Nancy had found him in the library just minutes after the incident? And why was he at Heights House way before the wedding was due to start?

As for motive, Nancy couldn't think of one, except that Freddy seemed to harbor some resentment about his cousin's wealth. Could he be trying to ruin her wedding day out of spite?

Nancy recalled Libby saying that the ghost had worn a long black velvet cape, and she decided to search the library for it. But after a few moments of looking, she had turned up nothing.

"I'd better get upstairs and see how Libby is doing," she said to herself.

Out in the hall, she ran into Mandy. "Oh, Nancy, there you are. Libby is talking about canceling the wedding!" Mandy said breathlessly.

"What? Why?" Nancy asked.

"It's this ghost business," Mandy said, running her hands through her hair. "Libby told me all about it. It has her totally spooked. On top of that, about five minutes ago, her fiancé called in. It turns out that Charles was asleep when Tyler, the best man, went to get him."

"Isn't that *good* news?" Nancy said, confused. "Shouldn't Libby be happy that Charles didn't stand her up?"

"Actually, she's furious with him that he almost slept through their wedding," Mandy replied with a sigh. "He has a reasonable excuse. He's a medical intern, and he hadn't slept in two days."

"Oh, boy," Nancy murmured. As quickly as possible she told Mandy about the secret passageway. "I think someone dressed up as a ghost to try to scare Libby," she finished. "The question is who? And why?" Nancy didn't mention her encounter with Freddy Ewing or her suspicions about him. She didn't want to start pointing fingers without proof.

17

"We'd better report the incident to Rafe—he's our security guard," Mandy murmured. "His office is in the basement. And after that we should go up and talk to Libby."

Nancy glanced around. "Where are George and Bess?"

"George is in the chapel setting up the candles and flowers," Mandy replied. "Bess is in Libby's room cleaning up the broken vase."

The two of them headed down to the basement. Along the way, they passed the musicians hired for the reception and a man delivering the wedding cake. Mandy spoke to all of them briefly and marked some things down on her clipboard. Then she and Nancy proceeded to the security guard's office.

It was a small room with dingy yellow walls and a bare overhead light. A short, well-built man was sitting at a desk, facing the wall. The sign on the door said Rafe Kiernan, Security Guard.

"Rafe? It's me, Mandy."

The man turned around. He had a blond crew cut and piercing blue eyes and appeared to be in his late twenties. "Hi, there," he said. "Can I help you with something?"

Mandy introduced Nancy and Rafe. Then Nancy told Rafe about Libby's sighting of the ghost and the secret passageway.

"I didn't know about the passageway," Rafe said when Nancy had finished. He scratched his head. "I'll look around and see if I can't find this ghost, whoever he is."

"Please don't bother the bride, whatever you do," Mandy said quickly. "She's kind of, um, upset right now, understandably. And please don't question any of the guests. We don't want to ruin the wedding for anyone."

"If there *is* a wedding," Nancy said. "Maybe we'd better head upstairs and see what's going on with Libby and Charles."

The wedding march from Wagner's *Lohengrin* swept majestically through the halls of Heights House. Bess, George, and Nancy peeked into the chapel, where Libby was making her way up the aisle toward the altar. She looked beautiful in her ivory-colored Victorian gown and veil. The groom looked handsome in his black tuxedo with tails. The room was filled with flickering candles and bouquets of fragrant white roses.

"I'm so glad Libby decided to get married after all," Bess whispered. "It must have been the pep talk Mandy gave her."

"Don't forget Nan here, who managed to convince Libby that the ghost she saw wasn't really a ghost at all," George said in a low voice.

The music stopped and the minister began: "Dearly beloved, we are gathered here today to witness the union of Charles Cox Gibbons and Elizabeth Jenkins Ewing."

19

"We'd better get back to work," Nancy whispered to her friends. "Mandy said that she wanted us to double-check all the place settings for the reception."

Bess closed the chapel door quietly, and the three girls headed toward the ballroom. On the way, they ran into Mandy, who was carrying a heavy-looking carton. "Do you need some help with that?" Nancy called out to her.

Mandy shook her head. "Have you guys done the place settings yet? Because if you have, I have another job for you."

"We're on our way to do that now," George told her. "Or maybe we could split up, and one or two of us could tackle the place settings."

"Good idea." Mandy paused and readjusted the case in her arms. Then she nodded toward a small foyer. "The ballroom is right through there. George and Bess, why don't you deal with the place settings? Nancy, you can come with me and— Oh, no!"

Nancy stared at her, concerned. "What is it, Mandy?"

Mandy set the case down on the floor with a thud. She pointed to a bare table in the foyer. "There used to be a pile of wedding gifts there," she said. "They're gone!"

3

The Thief Gets Away

Bess's jaw dropped. "Gone? You mean, the wedding presents were *stolen?*" she asked incredulously.

Mandy rushed up to the table and ran her hands over it. "There were at least twenty or thirty gifts here as of a few minutes ago," she said frantically. "I had the guests put them here as they came through the front door. What on earth could have happened to them?"

Nancy glanced down the hallway and saw it was empty. Then she hurried through the foyer and into the ballroom. There she caught sight of a dark-haired man disappearing through a doorway. He was carrying a bulky pillowcase over his shoulder.

"Stop!" Nancy yelled, and raced after him. She

reached the doorway on the other side of the ballroom. It led to a set of stairs going up to the second floor. The man was almost at the top of the flight.

Nancy started up the stairs two at a time. The man glanced over his shoulder and flung the bulky pillowcase down at her. It hit her in the head.

The impact knocked Nancy off her feet. She tumbled down the stairs and landed flat on her back. Stunned, she lay there silently for a moment. Then she groaned and rubbed her head.

She sat up slowly. Nothing seemed to be broken, although she could feel some tender spots where she knew nasty bruises would be forming. She glanced around. There were gift-wrapped boxes everywhere, and the thief was gone.

Bess, George, and Mandy came rushing through the doorway. Bess knelt down beside Nancy, her blue eyes full of worry. "Nan, are you okay? What happened?" she demanded.

Nancy grabbed Bess's arm and rose to her feet. She felt slightly dizzy, but otherwise she seemed to be fine. "There's no time to waste," she said quickly. "Bess, George, come with me. The thief is on the second floor somewhere. Mandy, stay here and keep an eye on the gifts."

Before anyone could stop her, Nancy started up the stairs again. Bess and George looked at each other, shrugged, then followed their friend.

Up on the second floor, the three of them searched all the rooms. Like the Gold Room and the Blue Room, each room had a single color scheme and was elaborately decorated with Victorian furnishings.

"What did he look like?" George asked Nancy as they swept through the Green Room.

"He had dark hair," Nancy replied. "And I think he was dressed in a black tuxedo. But that's about all I noticed about him."

Nancy, Bess, and George combed the entire second floor, then headed downstairs. Nancy was pretty sure that the man was gone. Still, she and her friends checked out all the first-floor rooms, just to be certain.

When they got to the chapel, Nancy opened the door a crack and peered in. Libby, Charles, and all their attendants were still at the altar. The ceremony seemed to be winding down, however; the minister was delivering the blessing.

"Charles and Libby: May you perform and keep the vows and covenants made between you," he said, smiling at the couple. "May you love, honor, and cherish each other, and so live together in faithfulness and patience, in wisdom and true godliness, that your home may be a haven of blessing and a place of creativity and peace."

Nancy's gaze shifted from the minister to Libby's cousin Freddy, who was sitting in the back row by himself. That's strange, she thought. Why isn't he sitting with his family? Then she thought about the thief's appearance. Freddy had dark hair, and he, too, was wearing a tuxedo.

Bess tugged at Nancy's sleeve. "We'd better get back to Mandy," she whispered.

"Good idea," Nancy whispered back. "She's probably wondering where we are."

They found Mandy in the foyer, rearranging the gifts on the table. "Did you catch the thief?" she asked them immediately.

"I'm sorry, but he got away," Nancy said apologetically. "He had too much of a lead."

Mandy sighed and shook her head. "I don't understand what's going on," she said slowly. "First a ghost and now a thief. It's as if this wedding is cursed or something."

"It's more like someone is out to sabotage it," Nancy told her. "My guess is that the ghost and the thief are the same person." Maybe Freddy Ewing, she thought. Or maybe someone else altogether.

Mandy frowned, then glanced at her watch. "I want to get to the bottom of this, but there isn't time. The reception is going to start in about fifteen minutes, and there are a million things to do. I'm afraid we'll have to put our ghost- and thief-catching on hold."

"Absolutely," Nancy said, nodding. "What do you want us to do?"

"Well, there are the hors d'oeuvres," Mandy began.

"Yum!" Bess said appreciatively. "What kind?"

George looked at her cousin in exasperation. "I think she wants us to help prepare them, Bess, not eat them," she said. "Which way is the kitchen?"

"Put these cucumber sandwiches on the silver trays," Daphne Applebaum said. "The clam canapés go on the big platters with the little pink roses on them." She made a face. "Or maybe not. Maybe they'd look better on the Limoges china. What do you guys think?"

Daphne was Mandy's younger sister, and the owner of a new catering business called Incredible Edibles. She was preparing the food for the four weddings at the mansion.

As Nancy sliced cucumbers, she watched Daphne work. She noticed how different Daphne seemed from Mandy. First of all, Daphne was short and plump and had sun-streaked brown hair that fell down her back in a wild cascade of curls. And while Mandy was nervous and energetic, Daphne was slow and relaxed, almost to a fault. A reception for a hundred and fifty people was about to start and she had yet to shift into high gear.

"It must be great to be a caterer," Bess told Daphne as she arranged the clams on a platter. "I mean, you get to cook all this yummy food, plus go to fancy weddings and parties and stuff."

"Actually, it's kind of a drag," Daphne admitted. "It's hard work and high pressure, too." She added, "To tell you the truth, I miss my old job."

"What was that?" George asked.

"I was a carpenter," Daphne replied. "Well, more of an assistant carpenter. I helped build houses." She grinned. "And before that, I did a bunch of other things. I was a waitress, singer, car mechanic, painter, word processor, gardener, paralegal . . . have I left anything out? Oh, yeah, pet sitter."

"You did all that?" Bess asked.

Mandy came running into the kitchen. "There's no punch on the buffet table," she said frantically. "Where is the punch, Daphne? The receiving line is forming, and the guests will start heading over to the ballroom in about five minutes."

"Oh, yeah, the punch." Daphne nodded at a massive crystal punch bowl that was sitting on the counter. "Nancy and George, could you guys take that into the ballroom? Oh, and put some flowers or something around the base of it.

26

Thanks a lot." She glared at Mandy. "Anything else I can do for you, boss?"

"Daphne!" Mandy exclaimed. "Just because I'm your sister doesn't mean you can—" She glanced at Nancy and her friends and stopped. "This isn't the time," she said curtly to Daphne. "We have a million things to do."

Nancy and George exchanged puzzled looks, then Nancy went over to the punch bowl and picked it up. "We'll be right back," she told Daphne.

As she and George left the kitchen, Nancy overheard Mandy reprimanding Daphne for wearing her hair down. "I've told you before. You have to put it back in a ponytail or up in a hairnet when you work around food," she said sternly.

"Is it my imagination or is there a little tension between Daphne and Mandy?" George whispered to Nancy when they were out in the hallway.

"I think you're right," Nancy whispered back. "I wonder what's going on between them?"

Nancy carried the punch bowl into the ballroom. She hadn't had a chance to study the room earlier, when she was chasing the thief. It was enormous and elegant, with balconies, crystal chandeliers, floor-to-ceiling windows covered with red velvet drapes, and murals depicting

Greek gods and goddesses. Dozens of tables were set up with white linen tablecloths, antique place settings, candles, and flowers.

Nancy set the punch bowl down on the buffet table. "Daphne said to put flowers around the base," Nancy reminded George. "But she didn't say where we were supposed to get them."

"I think there are some odds and ends up in the Blue Room," George said. "Why don't I go up and get them right now?"

George headed upstairs, and Nancy went back to the kitchen, where Mandy, Daphne, and Bess were putting the finishing touches on the hors d'oeuvres. Nancy noticed that Daphne had her hair pulled back in a ponytail.

"We were just telling Daphne about the ghost and the thief," Mandy told Nancy.

"I think it's kind of exciting," Daphne said, her brown eyes twinkling. "You know, it shakes things up a bit. I mean, who wants a wedding with no mishaps, right?" When Mandy frowned at her, Daphne added, "I'm just kidding, Mandy. Don't be so serious all the time."

Mandy started to say something to her sister, but stopped herself and turned her attention to Nancy instead. "I just remembered, you're a detective, aren't you?" she said.

"Well, I've solved a few cases," Nancy said.

"A *few* cases!" Bess repeated in amazement. "Are you kidding? Nancy's solved dozens. And I bet she could solve the mystery that's going on right here in Heights House. Couldn't you, Nan?''

Nancy was about to reply when something caught her eye. There was a fleeting, shadowy movement in the kitchen doorway. Somebody was eavesdropping!

4

Out of Control

Nancy leaned toward Bess. "Talk about something, anything," she whispered. "And raise your voice a little."

"Uh, okay, whatever," Bess murmured, bewildered. "Uh, so, as I was saying, I saw this really cool movie last night," she said, more loudly. *"Revenge of the Ant-Eating Vampires.* Has anyone else seen it?" Mandy and Daphne gave her puzzled looks.

While Bess continued to chatter about the fictional movie, Nancy slipped quietly toward the doorway. The shadowy figure was no longer there. Nancy hurried into the hallway and looked to her left. Freddy Ewing was walking briskly toward the exit.

Nancy felt a tingle of excitement. Freddy again!

"Excuse me. Freddy Ewing, right?" she called out, rushing up to him.

Freddy stopped and turned around. "Are you following me? What do you want?"

"What do *you* want?" Nancy replied. "You seemed to be very interested in what was going on in the kitchen just now. Did you need something?"

Freddy narrowed his eyes at Nancy, then took a few steps toward her. Before she could move away, he grabbed her arm roughly. "I've had it with your nosy questions," he said in a low, threatening voice. "What is your problem, anyway? Isn't the wedding consultant keeping you busy enough?"

Staring at him levelly, Nancy shook her arm free. "I don't appreciate eavesdroppers," she shot back. "Someone was listening to our conversation in the kitchen, and I believe it was you."

"Well, it wasn't," Freddy retorted. "I was just cruising the hall, looking for a pay phone."

Nancy studied his face. She couldn't tell if he was lying or not. "I think there's one near the chapel," she said after a moment.

"I'm going to use my aunt's car phone. Excuse me." Freddy stalked off and went out the door.

The best man, Tyler Fitch, raised his champagne glass high in the air. "I want to make a toast to the bride and groom, Charles and

31

Libby," he said, smiling. "May they have a life-time of happiness together. And may Libby buy herself a good pair of earplugs so she doesn't have to listen to Charlie's awful snoring. Ha, ha, just kidding, man."

The crowd broke into laughter as Charles, who was tall, blond, and handsome, pretended to throw a punch in Tyler's direction. Tyler pretended to throw a punch back, then went on with his toast.

Holding her tray at her side, Nancy leaned against a column and glanced around the ballroom. So far the reception was going smoothly. The guests, many of whom were dressed in Victorian garb, seemed to be enjoying themselves. Daphne's Victorian dinner, which consisted of oyster bouillon, lobster Newburg, sweetbread patties, and asparagus salad, was a big success.

Nancy, George, and Bess, who had changed into high-necked gray maids' dresses right before the reception, had been working steadily, serving drinks and hors d'oeuvres, setting up the buffet table, clearing plates. Nancy had tried to keep an eye out for Freddy Ewing, but it wasn't easy. The room was crowded, and she was very busy.

Now, as Tyler finished his toast to Charles and Libby, Nancy scanned the room and tried to find Freddy among the tables. She thought she saw him sitting between two middle-aged women, but it was hard to be sure.

"Do you think the bride and groom would mind if I started dancing on the tabletops?"

Nancy turned around. An attractive young man, maybe twenty or twenty-one, was standing behind her, a big grin on his face. Dressed in a black tuxedo, he had wavy brown hair and a light smattering of freckles across the bridge of his nose.

"Excuse me?" Nancy said.

"It's just that I'm bored," the man said cheerfully. "Don't you find weddings boring?"

"Actually, I'm—" Nancy began.

"Oh, I'm sorry, I didn't even introduce myself. Where are my manners?" The man thrust his hand out. "Kevin Royko, at your service."

Nancy gave Kevin her hand. He bowed over it with a dramatic sweep of his arm and kissed it lightly. Nancy grinned and withdrew her hand. "Are you a friend of the groom or bride?" she asked him.

"Both," Kevin replied promptly. "Lucky me, huh? And what about you?"

Nancy pointed to her tray. "I work here," she said.

"Nan! Nancy!"

Nancy glanced over Kevin's shoulder. Bess was standing a little way off, waving her arms frantically and calling out to her.

Nancy turned to Kevin. "Excuse me, but I'm being summoned. It was nice meeting you."

"The pleasure was all mine," Kevin said, his blue eyes twinkling. "If you see someone moonwalking on the buffet table later on, you'll know it's me."

Nancy smiled at him and hurried toward Bess. What a strange guy, she thought.

Bess intercepted her and steered her toward the kitchen. "Major disaster with the wedding cake," she whispered fiercely. "The wrong cake was delivered, and there isn't enough time to get the right one here."

"Oh, no," Nancy said, alarmed. Then a thought occurred to her. "Wait a second, though. Can't we just use the wrong cake?"

"Wait till you see it," Bess said, rolling her eyes. "By the way, who was that cute guy you were talking to?"

Nancy laughed. "One of the guests. I'll introduce you later, if you want."

In the kitchen Mandy and Daphne were standing over the cake, having a heated discussion. George was hovering behind Mandy, stirring something in a bowl.

Nancy glanced at the cake. Bess was right; it was never meant for an elegant Victorian wedding. A large sheet cake with yellow frosting, it was decorated with sugary white baseballs and

34

bats and the words Congratulations, River Heights Raccoons!

Mandy groaned and said, "Somewhere in River Heights, a bunch of eight-year-old softball players are enjoying a three-hundred-dollar Victorian wedding cake. How did this happen?"

"Maybe we could convince Libby and Charles that baseball bats and balls are Victorian wedding symbols," Daphne said.

Mandy glared at Daphne. "Don't be ridiculous, Daph. Besides, I hired this new baker on your recommendation. This is all your fault!"

"*My* fault? You're the one who signed for the delivery. You should have been able to tell from the shape of the box that something was wrong," Daphne retorted.

"The question is, what are we going to do?" Nancy asked.

Mandy turned her attention back to the cake. "I had a problem similar to this once. Not nearly as bad, of course," she added, frowning at Daphne. "But still, we might be able to salvage this cake."

"How?" George asked her.

"There's no time to change the shape of it and refrost the entire thing," Mandy explained. "But we can remove the decorations, smooth out the writing with a rubber spatula, and kind of cover the whole thing up with slivered almonds and fresh flowers." She glanced at Nancy, George, and Bess. "Come on, let's get busy."

Twenty minutes later Nancy, George, and Bess carried the redecorated cake into the ballroom. Mandy had done a wonderful job with the almonds and fresh flowers, and neither Libby nor Charles seemed to think anything was amiss as Nancy and her friends set the cake down in front of them. The couple sliced the cake and fed each other the first small bites, and the guests broke into delighted applause.

"Whew," George said as she, Nancy, and Bess headed back to the kitchen. "Mandy saved the day!"

"I told you she was good," Bess said. "When I get married, I may hire her as my wedding consultant," she added dreamily. "I can see it now. We'll have a medieval theme, and I'll wear a puffy velvet dress and one of those tall cone hats. My fiancé will wear a suit of armor. As for the menu, we'll have lots of roast mutton or something."

Nancy was about to say something when she noticed Rafe, the security guard, standing near a ballroom doorway.

Nancy introduced him to George and Bess. "Any news?" she asked him.

"About that ghost business, I searched everywhere twice, but I didn't find anyone acting, you know, suspicious." He ran a hand through his short blond hair. "Checked out the secret passageway, too. Boy, what a weird place."

"I know it," Nancy said. Then she told Rafe about the near-theft of the wedding gifts. "I think it might be the same person, but I'm not sure," she finished. "In any case, you should keep your eyes open for the rest of the evening. Mandy spoke to Libby and Charles, and they don't want the police called in. So it's up to us to make sure there's no more trouble."

"No problem," Rafe said, nodding. Then he stared for a moment at Libby and Charles, who were holding hands and kissing. "Great wedding, huh?" he said. "Nice couple. They deserve a spread like this. It's the most important day of their lives, right?"

Nancy followed Rafe's gaze. Despite all the minor and major mishaps this evening, the wedding had taken place, and Libby and Charles seemed happy. Still, Nancy couldn't help wondering if Freddy—or whoever was behind the ghost incident and the attempted theft of the gifts—was going to strike again. There was the rest of the night, and the next day the bride and groom were off to honeymoon in Maine. Would the culprit follow them there?

The next morning Nancy woke to the sound of thunder. She sat up in her bed, stretched, and glanced outside. The sky was almost black, and rain was coming down in torrents. Just outside her window, the branches of a maple tree trembled and shook in the wind. "Oh, no," she breathed. "The wedding."

Nancy peered at her alarm clock; it was a few minutes before six. The second wedding of the weekend was starting in four hours, and worse luck, it was an outdoor wedding. The ceremony was to take place in the gazebo behind Heights House, and the brunch reception was to be on the back lawn.

Nancy swung her slender legs over the edge of the bed, slipped on her robe, and trotted downstairs. She found her father, Carson Drew, eating breakfast in the dining room.

Carson looked up from his bowl of cereal. He had brown hair that was graying at the temples and blue eyes just like Nancy's. "Good morning, honey. Did you sleep well?" he asked her.

Nancy bent down and kissed him on the cheek. "Like a rock," she replied.

Hannah Gruen popped her head in the doorway. She had been the Drews' housekeeper for many years, but Nancy thought of her as much more than a housekeeper. Hannah had been like a mother to her since Nancy's mother had died when she was three.

"Can I interest anyone in pancakes?" Hannah called out. "It seems like a pancake sort of morning."

"Oh, I guess I'll take a short stack, if you're making them," Carson said cheerfully. "I can never say no to pancakes."

"Neither can I." Nancy sat down, poured herself a glass of orange juice from a pitcher, and gulped it down. "Besides, I have another wedding at Heights House in a few hours, and I'll need my energy," she added.

"Heights House," Carson murmured. "You know, there was some sort of big controversy surrounding that place years ago. I can't remember what it was now."

"Did it have to do with one of your clients?" Nancy asked him curiously. Her father was a lawyer.

Carson shook his head. "No. I think it was something I read in the paper, or maybe something I heard."

"You know, I went to high school with a woman who used to live there," Hannah spoke up. "Grace Merrill. But I lost track of her many years ago."

"Grace Merrill," Nancy repeated thoughtfully. "There are two portraits in the front hall of the house. Bess said they were of Joseph and Jeanine Merrill, the original owners of the house. They must be Grace Merrill's relatives."

"Joseph and Jeanine Merrill were probably Grace's grandparents," Hannah said.

Hannah disappeared into the kitchen to make

the pancakes. Nancy poured herself more juice and told her father about the strange incidents at Libby and Charles's wedding.

"I don't like the sound of that, Nancy," Carson said gravely when she'd finished. "This person could be dangerous."

"Well, now that Libby and Charles's wedding is over, I hope he's out of the picture," Nancy told him. "I was a little worried that he might follow Libby and Charles to Maine. But I talked to Libby after the reception, and she said that they're honeymooning in some top secret place. So I doubt this guy could find them, even if he wanted to."

"Still, be careful the rest of this weekend, okay?" Carson said, his blue eyes full of concern. "You never know if this guy might come back to Heights House, for whatever reason."

Nancy turned her windshield wipers off, seeing that the rain had let up. Mandy had called while Nancy was eating breakfast and asked her to come in earlier than planned to help set up inside in case the rain continued. Nancy was on her way to pick up Bess and George. The three of them planned to head out to Heights House together.

Nancy reached over and turned on the radio. "This is WRIV, River Heights's favorite rock and roll source," a deep male voice boomed. "Still cloudy out there, folks, with scattered showers. The weatherman says that it might clear up later, though. So stay tuned, and stay dry."

A loud rock song began to play. Nancy turned the volume down slightly. A car passed her on the left and sped off, splashing her windshield with mud. "Oh, great," she muttered. She turned on the switch for the windshield cleaning fluid.

What came out was not windshield cleaner but something else altogether. A thick, red liquid sprayed out, and the wiper blades smeared it across the windshield. Nancy couldn't see the road at all. She pumped the brake pedal a few times to warn any driver in back of her, then slammed on the brakes.

The car fishtailed wildly, tossing Nancy from right to left within her seat belt. She tried to straighten out the Mustang, but she couldn't see the road, and with a panicky feeling in her stomach, she realized she was about to lose control of the car!

5

Family Tensions

Nancy let up on the brake and began tapping on it lightly, trying to get the car to slow down gradually on the slippery road. She wished she could see; she was on a narrow street, and she could have been on the brink of crashing into a tree or a building or another car.

Nancy rolled down the window on the driver's side and stuck her head out, all the while keeping her right hand on the steering wheel and her right foot on the brake. She saw in an instant that she had crossed over to the left side of the street, and a pair of headlights was coming at her from the opposite direction. She was about to have a head-on collision!

Nancy sucked in a terrified breath and spun the steering wheel to the right. Her car careened into the right lane seconds before the other car sped by her, the driver honking angrily. Nancy began tapping on the brakes again, and her car slowed to a stop.

She shifted into park and leaned back in her seat, feeling exhausted. "That was way too close," she murmured grimly to herself.

After recovering her composure, Nancy turned on the hazard lights, got out of the car, and opened up the hood. The rain had started up again and began to soak her hair and clothes. She saw that the windshield cleaning fluid tank was filled with red liquid. It looks like paint, she thought. Someone put paint in the tank deliberately to make me get into an accident. What is going on? She left the hood up as a sign of distress and got back into the Mustang. Her hands were shaking as she rolled up the window and locked the door. She realized that someone had to be very sneaky and very determined to put the paint in her car without her noticing. And that someone was still out there . . . somewhere.

Half an hour later, as a tow truck drove away with Nancy's blue Mustang, she slid into the front seat of George's car. The cousins had come to her rescue as soon as Nancy had called from a nearby pay phone.

"Are you *sure* you're okay?" Bess asked from the backseat. "You look awful."

"Thanks a lot," Nancy said with a grin. "I'm fine—just a little shaken up."

George started the car. "Who do you think could have done it?"

Nancy rubbed her hair with a towel that Bess had brought. "My guess is that it's connected to the stuff that happened at Libby and Charles's wedding," she said slowly. "But what could be the motive? Was the person worried that I was onto him?"

By the time they got to Heights House, the rain had stopped. Nancy went into the mansion briefly to change into her uniform of black pants, white blouse, and black bowtie, then went out back to join the others.

Nancy was awed by the beauty of the grounds behind the mansion. There were acres of perfectly landscaped gardens—rose gardens, herb gardens, perennial gardens, and more— bordered by a vast forest of pine trees. There was also a small duck pond and a large, old-fashioned-looking gazebo near the edge of the woods. The gazebo was round with open sides and ornate wooden trim bordering the roof. Because of the rain, the air smelled sweet and fresh and cool. The sun was shining weakly through the clouds, which were moving east.

Bess, George, and Mandy were at the gazebo, decorating it with white paper wedding bells, woven baskets, African masks, and garlands of flowers. When Mandy saw Nancy heading their way, she rushed over to meet her. She was dressed in khaki slacks and a pale pink blouse.

"Bess and George told me what happened on your way here, Nancy," Mandy said anxiously. "Are you okay?"

"I'm fine," Nancy said. "Although now that someone is after me, too, I'm more eager than ever to catch the person."

"I am, too. And besides"—Mandy paused and glanced over Nancy's shoulder—"Oh, dear, we'll have to postpone this conversation," she said in a low voice. "The bride and her parents are here."

Nancy turned around. Walking toward them from the front of the house was a short, pretty woman in her early twenties. Her black hair was elaborately braided and pinned up on her head and she was wearing a crimson dress that set off her ebony skin. With her were a tall, broad-shouldered man with wire-rimmed glasses, and a petite woman with long, gray-streaked black hair in a ponytail.

"I nearly had a heart attack when I woke up this morning and saw it was raining like that," the young woman called out to Mandy. She smiled warmly at Nancy and her friends. "Hi, I'm Kanisha Partridge, and these are my parents, Jamal and Selma Partridge."

Nancy, Bess, and George introduced themselves. "It's great how the sun's coming out just in time," Nancy said to Kanisha.

"It must be a good omen for your wedding," Bess added.

Mr. Partridge cleared his throat and was about to say something when his wife elbowed him in the side.

Kanisha glanced at her father and her smile wavered. "Yes, I'm sure you're right, Bess," she said, her amber eyes still on her father. "It's definitely a good omen for my wedding."

"Your dress is hanging upstairs in the Gold Room," Mandy said quickly, as if to change the subject. "It looks gorgeous. The bright colors edged in gold are beautiful."

"Chantelle is a fabulous designer," Mrs. Partridge declared. She put her hand on her husband's arm. "Come on, Jamal. Let's walk around the grounds and look at the roses. You love roses."

"In a minute," Mr. Partridge said gruffly. "I left something in the car—I'll be right back." With that, he strode toward the parking lot.

Mrs. Partridge frowned as she watched him go. Then she turned to her daughter. "He'll be fine, honey," she said, sounding a little uncertain. "Why don't *we* walk around the grounds a bit? It'll help calm our nerves."

"All right, Mama," Kanisha told her. "And then I want to go up and look at my dress."

When mother and daughter had left, George frowned at Mandy. "What was that all about?"

Mandy sighed heavily. "It's Mr. Partridge," she said after a moment. "He's opposed to this wedding."

"He is? Why?" Bess asked.

"He doesn't like Kanisha's fiancé, Malcolm," Mandy explained. "Malcolm is a musician with no steady job, and Mr. Partridge doesn't think he's good enough for his daughter." She added, "I must say, Mr. Partridge's attitude has spoiled the entire wedding-planning process for Kanisha and Malcolm. It's terrible not having a parent's blessing on the most important day of your life."

Nancy was silent as she reflected on Mandy's words. If she got married, she knew her father would support her choice of a husband one hundred percent. She couldn't imagine having the kind of conflict with him that Kanisha had with her father. She felt bad for the bride-to-be.

Mandy's voice cut into Nancy's thoughts. "Well, as usual, we have a million things to do. I'll finish up these decorations. Bess and George, why don't you set up the chairs for the ceremony? We'll need about seventy-five of them, and you'll find them in the storage room off the ballroom." Mandy turned to Nancy and said, "Why don't you go see if Daphne needs help in the kitchen?"

"No problem," Nancy told her.

After Mandy rattled off a few more instructions, the three girls headed toward the house. "I guess there's no such thing as a trouble-free wedding, huh?" George remarked.

"Definitely not," Bess said with conviction. "Although last night's was the worst, with the ghost and thief and everything. Kanisha's dad's grumpy mood can't beat that." She shuddered. "I wonder if the ghost will be back today?"

George rolled her eyes. "Bess, that *wasn't* a real ghost—"

"I know you and Nancy think that, but I'm not so sure," Bess said. "After all, this is a really old mansion. And who knows? Maybe it's haunted by Joseph and Jeanine Merrill, the original owners of Heights House."

"Sure," George said. "And pigs can fly."

Once inside, George and Bess headed toward the ballroom to get the chairs, and Nancy went to the kitchen. On the way, she passed Mr. Partridge talking on the pay phone near the chapel. He had his back turned to Nancy.

"If only there was some way I could stop this wedding," he was saying in a low voice. "I can't stand the idea of my little girl marrying that no-good bum."

Nancy frowned, then continued on her way. She couldn't believe Mr. Partridge was being so coldhearted about his daughter's wedding.

Just before she reached the kitchen, Nancy ran

into someone else. A middle-aged woman was in the hall, peering intently at a painting. Gray-haired and attractive, she was wearing a black pantsuit, matching hat, and dark glasses.

Nancy stared at her curiously. "Can I help you?"

The woman turned, startled. "Oh, hello. No, I was just studying this lovely painting. It's an original Winslow Homer. Did you know that?"

"No, I didn't know," Nancy said, smiling. "Are you here for the wedding?"

The woman frowned. "Wedding? Goodness, no. I'm just taking a little tour of the house." Her frown softened into a wistful smile. "I've always been very fond of it. There's no other house like it in River Heights, or anywhere in the world, as far as I'm concerned."

"It's definitely a beautiful house," Nancy agreed. "Still, the premises are closed this morning because there's a wedding going on. In fact, it's closed all weekend, because there are two more weddings scheduled. I think it'll be open to the public again on Monday, though." Nancy was beginning to warm up to this charming woman and didn't like asking her to leave.

The woman's face fell. "I did drive all the way out. Oh, well, never mind. I suppose I'll have to come back here on Monday." She gave Nancy a fluttery wave and turned toward the exit. "Good-bye, my dear. I hope you enjoy the wedding."

"Goodbye," Nancy said, and proceeded to the kitchen.

She found Daphne chopping a massive pile of green peppers. The caterer had the radio on, and a lively blues song was playing.

"Oh, good, George, you're here," Daphne said, wiping her brow with the back of her hand. "I could really use you. The electric chopper broke down."

"I'm Nancy. George is the tall one with the short brown hair." She smiled and asked, "So, what can I do?"

"I'm sorry, Nancy. I'm really stupid with names." Daphne handed Nancy a knife. "You can help me cut these peppers up. They're going into the frittatas."

Nancy began chopping the peppers. She loved the way they smelled. "What else are you making for the brunch?"

"It's a vegetarian menu, with Caribbean influences," Daphne answered. "For hors d'oeuvres, we're having okra fritters and grilled eggplant. And for the main course, there's heart of palm salad, black beans, fried plantains, coconut rice, and mango chutney, plus the frittatas."

"Stop. You're making me hungry," Nancy said enthusiastically. "For an ex-carpenter, you seem to know a lot about food."

Daphne chuckled. "I've always loved to eat and cook. I used to make a lot of meals for my family when I was growing up. Now I cook for myself and my friends all the time."

"When did you get the idea to go into the catering business?" Nancy asked her.

A strange expression crossed Daphne's face. "Actually, it wasn't my idea," she said vaguely.

Nancy was about to ask her what she meant when there was a knock at the kitchen door. A middle-aged man stood in the doorway with a clipboard in one hand and several white boxes tucked under his arms.

"Bonaparte Florists," he said briskly. "Where do you want these bouquets and boutonnieres?"

Nancy went over to him. "Could I see the original order?" she asked him. Because of the bouquet shortage the day before, she wanted to make sure all the flowers were there before signing off on the delivery.

The man showed it to her, and Nancy pored over it carefully. Then, after inspecting the bouquets and boutonnieres, she asked the man to take them upstairs to the Blue Room. "I'll show you where it is," she told him.

The two of them went out of the kitchen and headed up the back stairway to the second floor. The door to the Gold Room—the bridal dressing room—was ajar. Kanisha and her mother were probably inside, checking out her wedding dress, Nancy thought. Maybe they'd like to see the bridal bouquet.

"Hang on just a second," she said to the delivery man. Then she knocked on Kanisha's door.

There was no reply. Nancy pushed the door open slightly—and gasped.

Hanging on a rack in the middle of the room was Kanisha's wedding dress—or what remained of it. Someone had slashed it to shreds.

6

The Sabotage Continues

Nancy rushed into the Gold Room and looked around quickly. The room seemed to be empty. She checked the closet, just to be sure. Then she went over to the rack to inspect the damage to the bridal dress.

She could see that the dress had once been stunning—before it had been reduced to shreds. Gold woven ribbon trimming the bright red, gold, and purple fabric of the dress created a rich, shimmery effect. Kanisha would have looked beautiful in it, Nancy thought.

She fingered one of the slash marks. It was clean and neat, as though done by a sharp knife or a razor.

"Excuse me, but what do you want me to do

with these boxes?" the delivery man said impatiently.

Nancy glanced over her shoulder. "Oh, I'm sorry. Could you take them to the Blue Room? It's the last door on your right."

The delivery man left, and Nancy turned her attention back to the dress. Who could have done such an awful thing? Without the dress, there was no way Kanisha could go on with her wedding.

Then a terrible thought occurred to Nancy. She had heard Mr. Partridge telling someone on the phone that he wished he could stop his daughter's wedding. Could he have gone so far as to destroy Kanisha's dress?

"It's right in here," came the sound of Mandy's voice. "I know you're going to love it. Chantelle made some last-minute changes to the neckline, just as you wanted—"

Nancy whirled around. Mandy was walking through the door, followed by Kanisha and Mrs. Partridge.

Oh, boy, Nancy thought, poor Kanisha. She took a deep breath and said, "I'm afraid I've got some bad news—" Before she could go on, Kanisha ran up to the dress. "Is—is this my gown?" she gasped. "Wha—what happened?"

"I found it like this just now," Nancy said. "I'm really sorry, Kanisha."

Mandy shook her head. "It was fine when I was up here half an hour ago. I don't understand."

Kanisha looked as though she were about to faint. Mrs. Partridge took her arm and urged her into a chair. "You sit down, honey," she said gently. Then she turned to Mandy, her brown eyes blazing angrily. "This is all your fault! What kind of security do you have in this place, anyway? How could you people let some vandal in here to ruin my daughter's wedding dress?"

"There's a security guard on the premises, but he doesn't keep track of everyone who comes and goes," Mandy replied in a trembling voice. "I'm so sorry, Kanisha, Mrs. Partridge. I take full responsibility for this."

Kanisha began to cry. "What are we going to do, Mama?" she whimpered. "I can't get married without a dress."

"Is there any way you can get a replacement?" Nancy asked Mandy.

"A replacement?" Mandy echoed. Then her face lit up. "Yes, of course! Chantelle showed us a sample of a dress like this one, remember, Kanisha? It was trimmed with gold, except the design was a little different."

Kanisha got a handkerchief out of her purse and dabbed at her eyes. "I don't know," she said uncertainly. "Besides, what about the size?"

"All of Chantelle's samples are size eights, and

55

you're a size eight, right, Kanisha?" Mandy said eagerly. "I think this could work. Why don't I get her on the phone and see if she can messenger it over?"

Kanisha and her mother exchanged a glance. "All right," Kanisha said after a moment. "It's worth a try. Although it won't be the same as wearing my own dress."

"I know," Mandy said. "Again, my deepest apologies. Let me call Chantelle and we can talk about this some more."

"While you're talking to Chantelle, why don't I get Rafe to come up here?" Nancy asked Mandy. "We should report the incident to him."

Mandy nodded. "Good idea."

Nancy and Mandy left the room together, leaving Mrs. Partridge to comfort her daughter. As soon as they were in the hall, Mandy turned to Nancy.

"I can't take much more of this," Mandy said. "First, we have normal incidents—not enough flowers, the wrong wedding cake, a lipstick smear on Libby's dress, which she did herself. Okay, I can cope with all that, but then a 'ghost' shows up in Libby's closet, and her wedding gifts are almost stolen. On top of that, you almost get into an accident because someone sabotaged your car. And now this wedding dress disaster." She shook her head. "We'd better catch the person responsible before someone gets hurt or I lose all my clients, or both."

"I don't know if it's only one person," Nancy said. "I mean, at first I thought someone was after Libby and Charles. But why would that same person destroy Kanisha's wedding dress? It doesn't make sense."

Mandy sighed. "You're right. It doesn't."

Down in the basement, Nancy found Rafe in his office. He was sitting at his desk, staring thoughtfully at a photograph.

"Excuse me," Nancy said, rapping on his door, which was partially open.

Rafe turned around. "Oh, hi. It's Nancy, right?" he said pleasantly.

Nancy walked into the office and glanced briefly at the photograph. It was of a pretty, dark-haired woman. "Who's that?" she asked Rafe.

"That's Patricia, my fiancée," Rafe replied. "She's beautiful, isn't she? And boy, can she cook! Do you know what she makes me for dinner every Sunday? She makes this—"

"I'd love to hear about it, but maybe another time," Nancy said, smiling. "We've got some trouble upstairs."

"Huh? I'm sorry. Here I am going on." Rafe set the photograph down and rose from his chair. "Okay, what's the problem?" he asked, all business.

"Someone destroyed Kanisha Partridge's wedding dress," Nancy explained. "Come on. I'll fill you in on the way up."

Five minutes later Rafe and Nancy reached the Gold Room. Kanisha and Mrs. Partridge were there, along with Mandy, Mr. Partridge, George, and Bess.

Mandy turned to Nancy. "I was just telling the Partridges that Chantelle is coming right over with the replacement dress," she said. Nancy could tell that she was trying to sound cheerful.

Mrs. Partridge narrowed her eyes at Rafe. "Are you going to explain to us how some crazy vandal managed to get into this house and ruin my daughter's dress on her wedding day?"

"Two hours before a wedding, the doors are opened so that staff and guests are free to come and go," Rafe said. "It's our policy. We've never had any problems with vandals before."

As Rafe continued talking, Nancy watched Mr. Partridge closely. He was listening to Rafe with a blank expression; Nancy had no idea what he was thinking or feeling. She tried to imagine him taking a knife or a razor to his own daughter's wedding dress. Was he capable of such a sick act? How desperate was he to stop Kanisha from marrying Malcolm?

"Would you like to call the police and report this incident?" Rafe asked Kanisha.

Kanisha shook her head. "No police," she said

vehemently. "I'm getting married in forty-five minutes, and I don't want the police disturbing things."

"Forty-five minutes," Mandy repeated. She glanced nervously at her watch, then at her clipboard. "There're still a million things to do."

"If no one needs me for anything, I'm going out for a walk," Mr. Partridge said abruptly. Without waiting for a reply, he squared his shoulders and headed for the door.

I've got to follow him, Nancy thought. She had no proof he had sabotaged Kanisha's dress, but she didn't want to take the chance that he might try again to disrupt the wedding.

"Daphne needs me in the kitchen," Nancy said cheerfully. "I'll see you all later." Then, before anyone could say anything, she turned and followed Mr. Partridge out the door.

The ceremony began promptly at ten o'clock. Nancy and George stood near the house and watched as Kanisha and her fiancé, Malcolm Quinn, strolled hand in hand down a gravel path toward the gazebo. One of Malcolm's friends was playing a love song on the guitar. Nearly a hundred people stood on the lawn, watching the procession with happy smiles.

All except Mr. Partridge, Nancy noticed. He was standing up front with his arms crossed tightly over his chest and a grim expression on his face. Still, he wasn't disrupting the ceremony, and as far as Nancy could tell, he had no plans to do so. She had spent much of the last forty-five minutes following him, and all he had done was walk around and brood.

Nancy turned her attention back to the bride and groom. Kanisha looked beautiful in her replacement dress, which was similar to her original gown. And Malcolm, who was tall and slim, with long, corn-rowed brown hair, looked handsome in black pants, white collarless shirt, and cloth jacket. Kanisha had mentioned to Nancy that the Quinns were originally from Jamaica, and that she and Malcolm planned to honeymoon there.

"So far, so good," George said to Nancy in a low voice.

"So far," Nancy replied, nodding. "I wish we knew for sure who destroyed Kanisha's dress, though. I don't like thinking that our culprit is on the loose."

"Do you still suspect Kanisha's father?" George asked her. Nancy had filled Bess and George in on her doubts about Mr. Partridge.

"He's my only suspect so far. But I don't have any proof against him, and I'm having a hard time believing that he'd do that to his own daughter." Nancy smiled and gave a shrug. "But maybe I'm not being objective. Maybe I have too much faith in other people's fathers because *my* dad is so great."

The guitarist was winding down, and Kanisha and Malcolm were stepping up to the gazebo. Nancy glanced up; the sky was a bright blue, with a few wispy clouds. The cool, rain-washed breeze carried the scent of ceremonial incense from the gazebo.

Then Nancy glanced at the pine forest just beyond the gazebo and did a double take. She caught the fleeting movement of a figure behind a tree; it was wearing a long black cloak and had a skull's head. Nancy gasped. It was Libby's ghost!

The ghost emerged from behind the tree and seemed to look straight at Nancy through hollow eye sockets. In spite of herself, Nancy felt a chill go up her spine. Then the ghost raised one hand in the air and pointed a finger ominously at Kanisha and Malcolm.

Nancy tugged on George's arm and nodded toward the woods. "See over there?" she whispered urgently. "That's—"

A loud crash and a scream cut her off. The gazebo floor had collapsed beneath Malcolm and Kanisha, and the bride and groom disappeared before Nancy's eyes.

7

A New Suspect

More screams filled the air. Nancy and George took off running toward the gazebo. When they got there, Nancy assessed the situation quickly. A long, wide board in the middle of the gazebo floor had come loose, and Kanisha and Malcolm had fallen through the opening. Nancy frowned. The board had been fine an hour ago, when Mandy, George, and Bess were decorating the gazebo. Had someone tampered with it in the meantime?

Mr. and Mrs. Partridge, who'd gotten to the gazebo ahead of Nancy and George, were pulling Kanisha and Malcolm out of the hole. "Are you okay, Kanisha honey?" Mrs. Partridge asked anxiously.

Struggling to her feet, Kanisha looked slightly

shell-shocked. "I'm fine," she said, then turned to Malcolm. "What about you, sweetie? Are you all right?"

"I'm fine," Malcolm replied, brushing some dust off his slacks. "What happened, anyway? Didn't anyone check this thing before the ceremony?"

Mandy came rushing up to the gazebo. Bess was right behind her. "We saw what happened out the kitchen window," Mandy said breathlessly. "Are you both okay? I can't believe this happened. Is anybody hurt? How did this happen, anyway?"

Nancy's mind flashed back to the moment she'd heard Malcolm and Kanisha scream. Just seconds before, she'd spotted the ghost in the woods.

Nancy turned to George and grabbed her arm. "Come on!"

"Huh? What?" George asked. But Nancy had already taken off toward the woods beyond the gazebo.

"What's up?" George said when she'd caught up to Nancy. The edge of the woods was about a hundred feet from the gazebo, and Nancy was almost there.

"Just before I heard the crash, I saw the so-called ghost behind one of those trees," Nancy explained. "It was a person dressed in a skull's head mask and a long black cloak."

"You're kidding!" George exclaimed. "Do you think he or she was responsible for the gazebo mess?"

"It's possible." Nancy stopped at the pine tree where the ghost had been hiding. She glanced around the dense, sun-dappled woods. She couldn't see anyone, and the only sound she heard was the mournful cry of a bird.

George knelt on the ground. "Check this out, Nan!" she said, pointing to some footprints on the ground. "Looks like our ghost has big feet."

Nancy knelt down beside George and studied the footprints. Because the earth was muddy from the morning's storm, she couldn't make out any telling details, such as the shoe type. She looked around for more prints, but there were too many pine needles on the ground.

"This mystery gets weirder and weirder," Nancy remarked, standing up. "I thought Freddy Ewing was the ghost in Libby's closet yesterday and that he also tried to steal her wedding gifts."

"Freddy Ewing?" George echoed. "Who's Freddy Ewing?"

"Libby's cousin," Nancy replied. "But there was no way Freddy could be guilty of destroying Kanisha's dress, so I figured we were dealing with two different culprits—maybe Freddy and Kanisha's father." She frowned and shook her head. "But the fact that the ghost showed up yesterday and today, at Kanisha and Malcolm's wedding, complicates everything. Especially if he tampered with the floorboard."

"I get it," George said slowly. "You're thinking that we've got one culprit who tried to ruin both weddings."

Nancy nodded. "Right. And I don't think that either Freddy or Mr. Partridge fits the bill."

The wedding resumed a half hour later, after Rafe and Mandy had fixed the floorboard. The ceremony was brief but memorable, consisting of vows written by the bride and groom.

As they exchanged rings, Malcolm looked deeply into Kanisha's eyes and said, "Kanisha, I give you this ring as a sign of my love and faithfulness. With you, I've found my beginning: a place of peace from which every path leads forward. Like this ring, my love will encircle you and be with you always."

Kanisha replied, "Malcolm, I give you this ring as a sign of my love and faithfulness. With you, I've found my end: a place of joy as complete as this day. Like this ring, my love will encircle you and be with you always."

Nancy was with Bess, watching the proceedings from where they were setting up the stage for the band. Bess wiped away a tear, sniffed, and sighed.

Malcolm and Kanisha concluded the ceremony by jumping over a broom. "Why do they do that?" Bess asked Nancy.

"It's a tradition that goes back to the days of slavery in America," Nancy answered. "By law, Africans weren't allowed to marry. So young couples created their own wedding ceremony by jumping over a broom in front of their families and friends. It symbolized their step into matrimony."

"That's cool," Bess said, nodding. "You know, I've been giving *my* wedding a lot of thought. I think I'll scrap the medieval theme and do an international thing. I'll wear a silk kimono, my fiancé will wear a toreador outfit, we'll serve sushi and pasta and Mongolian hot pot and crêpes—"

"Oh, Bess." Nancy laughed.

"No, I'm serious!"

The ceremony over, Kanisha and Malcolm mingled with their guests around the gazebo. Nancy noticed Mr. Partridge off to the side, keeping to himself. She also noticed three teenage boys walking toward her and Bess at the bandstand. They were carrying big, beat-up leather cases.

"We're the band," one of the boys announced blandly to Nancy and Bess. "Where do we set up?"

Bess stared at him. "You're the band? I thought there were supposed to be eight of you."

The three boys looked at each other and laughed. "Yeah, right," the second one said. Then he scratched his head and frowned at Nancy and Bess. "This *is* Bobby Miller's birthday party, right?"

"Uh, no," Nancy replied. "This is the Partridge-Quinn wedding."

"Oh, man!" the third boy exclaimed, sounding annoyed. "Davey sent us to the wrong gig!"

"Who's Davey?" Bess asked him.

"Our booking agent," he replied.

Nancy turned to Bess. "I bet this Davey guy booked the other band, too. He must have switched them by accident."

"I'll get Mandy," Bess said. "She's going to freak!"

Bess rushed off toward the house, and the three boys followed her to use the phone. Nancy resumed working on the stage. From time to time, she found herself looking up at the woods. She couldn't help wondering if the ghost would make a repeat appearance.

If the ghost had tampered with the gazebo, then there was no way Mr. Partridge could be responsible, Nancy thought. He couldn't be in two places at once, and Nancy had seen him with the other wedding guests at the same instant she had spotted the ghost in the woods.

Was more than one person involved? Nancy wondered yet again. She went back to her theory that Freddy Ewing and Mr. Partridge were the culprits. However, that didn't explain the presence of the ghost at both weddings, unless the figure was a third, unrelated culprit working separately from Freddy and Mr. Partridge.

A voice interrupted her thoughts: "Fancy meeting you here!"

Nancy turned around. Kevin Royko, the young man who'd wanted to moonwalk on the tabletops at Libby and Charles's wedding, was standing behind her. He was wearing a light blue seersucker suit and a tie with cartoon ducks all over it.

"Another wedding?" Nancy asked him, surprised. "You're a popular guy!"

"Not popular enough," Kevin said with a grin on his freckled face. "I don't have a girlfriend, and it's tough coming to all these romantic weddings without a date."

Nancy got the feeling he was flirting with her. Trying to steer him off that course, she changed the subject. "How do you know Kanisha and Malcolm?" she asked him smoothly.

"Her parents and my parents are old friends," Kevin replied. He turned and nodded toward the gazebo. "Say, what did you think about that weird accident? That was crazy, huh?"

"I felt really bad for Kanisha and Malcolm," Nancy told him. "I'm also not sure it was an accident."

The other guests began strolling toward the reception area. Nancy realized that she had to get back to the house to help serve the hors d'oeuvres. "Excuse me," she said to Kevin. "It was nice talking to you, but the reception's starting, and I've got to get back to work."

"I'll see you around," Kevin said with a smile.

Nancy headed straight for the kitchen and found Bess, George, Mandy, and Daphne there. "My hors d'oeuvres are going to be all dried out," Daphne was complaining. "How could the ceremony run so late?"

"Your hors d'oeuvres are going to be fine," Mandy said, patting her on the shoulder. She saw Nancy and waved at her. "Bess filled me in on the band fiasco," she said. "I called the booking agent and straightened it out. The right band will be here in about half an hour. In the meantime, can you run out to my car and get the box of tapes sitting on my front seat? We can play them until the band is set up and ready to go."

"No problem," Nancy said. She got Mandy's car keys from her and went to the parking lot. She found the van right away and picked up the box of tapes from the front seat.

When Nancy straightened up she saw a familiar figure sitting in a silver station wagon in the next row of cars. Kevin Royko was in the passenger seat and a gray-haired woman was in the driver's seat. They appeared to be having an intense discussion about something.

Nancy squinted, trying to see the woman better. Then it came to her: It was the woman she'd seen in the house earlier, admiring the Winslow Homer painting. Now that the woman had her dark glasses off, she looked familiar. Was she a friend of Nancy's father? Or maybe an old neighbor? She racked her brain, but she couldn't figure it out.

"Okay, give it up, Drew," Nancy told herself. "Get these tapes back to Mandy."

She half walked, half ran back to the house, holding the box of tapes under her arm. Off in the distance, she saw the guests gathering in the reception area. Bess and George were passing out hors d'oeuvres and drinks.

A minute later, Nancy reached the kitchen. But just outside the doorway, she hesitated. Angry voices were coming from inside; Mandy and Daphne seemed to be arguing.

"This is not the time to be having this discussion," Mandy was saying in a furious whisper.

"As far as you're concerned, it's *never* the time," Daphne retorted hotly. "You just don't want to hear what I have to say. Well, here it is, plain and simple: Someday, maybe sooner than you think, you're going to regret everything you've ever done to me!"

Nancy was startled. Daphne appeared to be threatening Mandy. But why?

Then she had a sudden, disturbing insight. Could Daphne be the saboteur? Was she trying to bring down Mandy and her business by spoiling all the weddings?

8

Trapped!

Nancy mulled over this new possibility. Daphne seemed to bear a grudge against her older sister. Was she angry and troubled enough to try to ruin Mandy's business and two weddings—and to endanger Nancy's life as well?

"I don't have time for this, Daphne," Mandy said coldly. "I have work to do, and so do you. Please act like a professional and do your job, and don't make me regret that I hired you."

Without waiting for Daphne's reply, Mandy turned on her heel and left the kitchen. As she passed Nancy, she gave her a brief, tense nod. If she was surprised to see Nancy standing there, she didn't show it.

Nancy watched Mandy walk away, then entered the kitchen. Daphne was at the counter, aiming a cleaver at a pineapple. Her face was bright red, and she was muttering something to herself. The air was pungent with the smell of bitter chocolate.

Nancy wanted to find out what was going on with the sisters, but she wasn't sure how to proceed. "Um, Daphne?" she said finally. "Are you okay?"

"Okay? I don't think so." Daphne wiped her forehead with the back of her hand, then proceeded to slice the pineapple into quarters with four deft blows.

"I heard you and your sister talking," Nancy persisted.

Daphne glanced at Nancy. "Oh? What did you hear?" she asked, her eyes narrowing.

"I couldn't make out any words," Nancy said. "But it seemed as if the two of you were arguing."

Daphne stared at Nancy for a moment, then sighed. "We were definitely arguing," she said. "Mandy thinks she's Ms. Perfect Businesswoman, you know? And she's always tried to make me do things her way. So she practically forced me to start Incredible Edibles so that I would have what she called a 'respectable career.'"

Nancy frowned. "How did she force you?"

Daphne waved her hand dismissively. "Oh, I owed her some money . . . well, more like a lot of money. She told me that she would forget the debt if I quit my part-time job and started this business. She even offered to pay my start-up costs."

"Why does Mandy care so much about what you do for a living?" Nancy asked.

"I don't know—because she's a control freak?" Daphne shook her head in exasperation. "Whatever it is, I'm sick of it. I wish she'd leave me alone."

Nancy remembered that before becoming a caterer, Daphne had had a string of odd jobs, including carpenter and car mechanic. That meant she would know how to rig the gazebo floorboard so that it would collapse under Kanisha and Malcolm's weight. And she could also have replaced the windshield cleaner in Nancy's car with red paint.

On the other hand, the person Nancy had seen running off with Libby and Charles's wedding gifts was male. If Daphne was the guilty one, was it possible that she had an accomplice? Or was Nancy dealing with a bunch of unrelated culprits committing a bunch of unrelated crimes? The whole thing was getting very complicated.

Bess popped her head into the kitchen. "Hey, Nan?" she called out. "Mandy sent me to get those tapes from you."

"The tapes—oh!" Nancy glanced down at the box of tapes, which she was still holding in her hands. "I totally forgot about them. Here, I'll take them to Mandy myself."

Nancy said goodbye to Daphne, then followed Bess down the hall. Along the way, Nancy filled Bess in on her new theory about Daphne.

"Wow," Bess said in amazement when Nancy had finished. "Do you think Daphne would stab her sister in the back like that?"

"It's possible," Nancy replied. "Still, it *is* only a theory, so I don't want to mention it to Mandy yet." She added, "You've been working for Mandy for a few months now, right? Do you know anything about her relationship with Daphne?"

Bess shook her head. "Not really. I mean, this is Daphne's first weekend working for Mandy. Before that, Mandy might have mentioned Daphne's name once or twice, but that was about it."

"That's a bit strange," Nancy said, puzzled.

Bess looked thoughtful. "Wedding number three is tonight," she said. "If Daphne is guilty of messing up the first two weddings, do you think she'll try to mess up the next one, too?"

"If she's guilty, then definitely," Nancy said grimly. She paused and glanced at her watch. "That wedding starts at eight, and we're supposed to be here at six, right? Why don't we get here an hour early? We can take turns keeping an eye on Daphne, and on things in general."

"Sure," Bess said with a sigh. "My whole weekend is shot because of all these weddings, anyway. What's another hour?" She added, "By the way, I met that hunky guy you were talking to yesterday, Kevin something. He's really nice!"

Nancy nodded. "Kevin Royko. When did you meet him?"

"Just now, when I was going to get you. He came up to me, introduced himself, and asked me to dance. When I told him there wasn't any music, he said, 'So what? Who needs music?'" Bess giggled. "Isn't that funny?"

"He's definitely a funny guy," Nancy said.

"You know the controversy about Heights House that I mentioned earlier?" Carson Drew asked Nancy. "After you left this morning, I remembered what it was."

Carson paused and raised his mug to his lips. He and Nancy were sitting in the living room, drinking tea and eating some delicious cranberry muffins Hannah had baked. It was a little past four, and Nancy was taking a break before heading back out to Heights House for the third wedding of the weekend.

"Go on," Nancy told her father eagerly.

"It was something I read in the paper a while back," Carson explained. "In fact, I got so curious I went down to the library after lunch and

76

went through some back issues. I found what I was looking for right away."

He pulled a folded-up piece of paper out of his pocket. "I copied the article for you," he went on. "But I'll give you the gist of it. See, Heights House was built in 1886 by Joseph Merrill, a banker, and his wife, Jeanine. Until a few years ago, their granddaughter, Grace Merrill Sayer, and her husband, Isaiah Sayer, lived in it. Grace inherited the house from her parents, who inherited it from Joseph and Jeanine."

"Grace Merrill Sayer is the woman Hannah went to high school with, right?" Nancy said.

Carson nodded. "Apparently. Anyway, a few years ago, Isaiah and Grace made some bad business decisions, and the two of them ended up owing a lot of back taxes on the property. Eventually, the city was forced to take it over. Isaiah died in the middle of it all, and Grace launched a legal battle to retain ownership. But she lost her case—and the house."

"That's a tough break," Nancy said sympathetically.

"After the city assumed possession, they tried to auction it off," Carson went on. "But they didn't get any takers because the place is too expensive to maintain. So the city decided to refurbish it and rent it out for weddings and other social functions." He added, "They just started doing that this year, and from what I understand, it's a big success. They've got bookings well into the fall."

"I'm not surprised," Nancy remarked. "Heights House is beautiful."

The front door opened, and Hannah walked in. She had a bag of groceries in her arms. "Hi, you two," she called out cheerfully.

"Do you need help with the bags?" Nancy asked her.

"Nope, this is it," Hannah replied. "By the way, Nancy, did you get the phone message I left for you?"

Nancy shook her head. "What message?"

"Oh, dear," Hannah muttered. She disappeared into the kitchen, then came back out again. She held a piece of paper out to Nancy. "Mandy Applebaum called about an hour ago," she explained. "Instead of coming to Heights House at six to set up, she wants you, George, and Bess to swing by Fifty-five Excelsior Street to pick up some supplies for the wedding."

"Fifty-five Excelsior Street," Nancy murmured. "That's downtown somewhere, isn't it?"

"I think so," Hannah said. "By the way, have I met this Mandy person? She sounded familiar."

"She's called the house before," Nancy told her. "Maybe you recognized her voice."

Hannah went into the kitchen to put away the groceries, and Nancy turned her attention back to her father. "So that's the big controversy surrounding Heights House, huh?" she said thoughtfully. "Did the newspaper article say whatever became of Grace Merrill Sayer?"

"No," Carson replied. "But wherever she's living now, I'm sure it's not nearly as elegant as Heights House."

Half an hour later, Nancy, Bess, and George were heading to Excelsior Street in Bess's car. Nancy's car was still in the garage. It was late afternoon, but the sun was still shining brightly.

George had a street map draped across her lap. "I think we take the next left off Hawthorne Boulevard," she said.

Bess turned the blinker on. "I wonder what Mandy wants us to get on Excelsior Street?"

"Whatever it is, it must be heavy, since she wanted all three of us to deal with it," Nancy said.

Bess made the left off Hawthorne Boulevard and continued driving. As she drove, the neighborhood grew more and more desolate. There were vacant lots surrounded by wire-mesh fences and deserted-looking buildings with graffiti sprayed all over them. Hardly any people were in sight.

"Where *is* this place, anyway?" George muttered. "This is kind of a bad area."

Nancy pointed out the window. "Excelsior Street," she announced. "Bess, turn here."

Bess made the turn, and soon they found the building marked 55. It was an old run-down brick warehouse that took up half the block. There were no other buildings around, and Nancy saw no sign indicating what kind of business it was. Weeds grew everywhere, and the sidewalk was cracked.

Bess parked the car, and they got out. "I don't know," Bess said uncertainly. "This place is kind of creepy."

"Bess is right," George said. "This place is definitely creepy."

"We'll be quick," Nancy said decisively. She went up to the door, stepping over a broken glass bottle as she did so, and knocked. There was no answer.

Frowning, she turned the doorknob. The door opened, and she walked in. She was in a vast, empty warehouse. The floors were covered with dust, and no one was in sight.

George and Bess followed her. "Mandy obviously gave us the wrong address. We should find a pay phone and call her," George said uneasily.

"That's a good idea," Nancy said. "I saw one on Hawthorne, about three blocks back."

They turned and headed toward the front

entrance. But before they could get out, the door slammed shut.

"Hey, what's going on?" George exclaimed.

Bess ran up to the door and jiggled the knob. Then she whirled around, a terrified look in her eyes. "Nancy, George—it's locked! We're trapped in here!" she cried out.

9

The Black-and-White Ball

"What do you mean, we're trapped?" George stepped forward and steered Bess out of the way. "Here, let me try it."

George had no success, either. She rattled the knob, threw her weight against the door, and finally resorted to giving it a couple of powerful karate kicks. Nothing worked.

"I guess I need to hit the gym more often," she said breathlessly. "Do you have your lock-picking kit with you?"

Nancy shook her head. "No." She went up to the door, got down on her knees, and studied the knob carefully.

"The ghost must have followed us out here and locked us in," Bess said, looking around nervously.

Nancy heard a car being started. The sound wasn't coming from Excelsior Street, but from somewhere on the other side of the warehouse. Nancy jumped to her feet and ran across the vast floor to a grimy, many-paned window. She got there in time to see a rusty yellow car screeching down an alley.

Nancy squinted, trying to make out the license plate number. But the car was already too far away.

George and Bess ran up to her. "What's going on?" Bess asked Nancy.

"I think that was our so-called ghost, or one of the ghost's accomplices," Nancy said, pointing out the window. "My guess is that the person called and left the message with Hannah for us to come out here. Then, just as Bess said, he or she followed us to the warehouse and locked us in."

"I thought it was weird that Mandy would send us to this place," George said. "You know, Daphne could have called your house and pretended to be Mandy. The two of them have similar voices."

"That's true," Nancy agreed. "The question is, why would Daphne—or whoever it was—want to lock us in here?"

Bess glanced around nervously. "Here's a more important question. How are we going to get out?"

Nancy, Bess, and George spent the next hour

83

trying to find a way out of the warehouse. They couldn't break a window, since all the windows had security bars on them, and the other doors had chains and padlocks.

"We haven't tried screaming for help yet," Bess pointed out as Nancy and George searched the room for tools they could use to dismantle the security bars. She went up to one of the windows and began screaming, "Help! *Help!*"

"Hey, Bess? I don't think anyone's listening," George said. "We seem to be stuck in no-man's-land here."

Nancy picked up some rusty screws from the floor, stared at them helplessly, then let them fall to the ground. She was beyond frustrated. They were trapped in an abandoned warehouse in the middle of nowhere, and in the meantime whoever was responsible for the shenanigans at Heights House was probably setting a new plan in motion for the evening wedding.

Then Nancy noticed something she hadn't noticed before. The security bars on one of the windows seemed to be askew. She stepped forward to take a better look at the window, which was about four feet up the wall. Two of the bars were rusted through at the bottom.

"George! Bess! Here's our way out!" Nancy shouted.

As her friends rushed to her side, Nancy tugged at the window. It wouldn't budge. Frowning, Nancy peered at it closely. It was painted shut.

Nancy took off one of her shoes. "Stand back," she warned Bess and George.

Nancy took a few steps back, aimed, and threw her shoe at the dead center of the window. The window shattered and glass flew everywhere.

Then Nancy proceeded to brush away the shards that remained in the window. After a while, she was able to clear a big enough space to crawl through. "Okay, someone give me a lift," she called out.

George bent down and made a cup with her hands. Nancy took off her other shoe, stepped up on George's hands, and boosted herself onto the windowsill, being careful not to cut herself on any pieces of broken glass. Then she bent the corroded security bars back and wriggled through. Within minutes, she was out on the sidewalk.

Without wasting a second, Nancy swooped up the shoe she had thrown and hurried to the front door of the building and unlocked it. Bess and George were waiting for her with her other shoe.

"Nice going," George said. "If it hadn't been for your sharp eyes, we might have been stuck in there for days."

Bess's blue eyes widened. "Stuck in there for *days?* Bite your tongue, George!"

Nancy hooked her thumb at Bess's car. "Okay,

now that we're free, we have to get to Heights House ASAP," she said firmly. "Somebody wanted us out of the way tonight. We have to stop them before it's too late."

Once they reached Heights House, they found Mandy in the ballroom. She was standing on a ladder, hanging black and white silk streamers from the ceiling. Nancy knew that the reception was going to be a lavish banquet followed by a black-and-white ball.

When Mandy spotted Nancy and her friends, she climbed down the ladder and came rushing up to them. "Where have you been?" she asked them, sounding frantic. "It's after six, and there's a million things to do."

"I got a message from you a few hours ago, telling us to go to Fifty-five Excelsior Street to pick up some supplies," Nancy cut in quickly. "Except whoever called wasn't you. Fifty-five Excelsior was a deserted warehouse, and as soon as we got inside, someone locked us in. We had to break a window to get out."

"What?" Mandy cried out. Her brown eyes scanned Nancy and her friends anxiously. "I'm so sorry this happened to you. Are you all right?"

"We're fine," George reassured her.

"What did this person who called you sound like?" Mandy asked Nancy.

"Our housekeeper took the message, so I have

no idea," Nancy replied. "But whoever it was knew that we were supposed to be here at six."

Mandy looked thoughtful. "I can't imagine who would have known that besides the four of us," she murmured. "Oh, and besides Daphne, of course. She knows everyone's schedules."

Nancy, George, and Bess exchanged glances. "Where is Daphne, anyway?" Nancy asked Mandy.

"She's in the kitchen, working like mad on the food." Mandy dug into her pocket and pulled out a small and elegant menu. In ornate black script, it read:

Black Olives and Goat Cheese
Truffle and Shiitake Mushroom Pâté
Smoked Eel
Black Bean Soup with Crème Fraîche
Mussels in White Wine
Blackened Catfish
Arroz con Calamares en Su Tinta
(Squid and Rice)
Poulardes aux Fines Herbes
(Baked Chicken with Herbs)
Couscous with Currants
Marinated Eggplant in Yogurt
White Asparagus Salad
Coconut Sorbet
Black Forest Cake

George studied the menu and grimaced. "Um, it all sounds great except for the smoked eel and squid. Do people really eat that stuff?"

"Absolutely," Mandy said, nodding. "The squid dish is one of my favorites. The whole thing turns black from the squid ink."

"Squid ink?" Bess asked in a squeaky voice.

Mandy stuffed the menu back into her pocket. "Daphne is really nervous about tonight, and so am I," she said. "The bride and groom, Bettina Li and Stone Hanson, are from New York City. She's an editor for a big fashion magazine, and he runs an art gallery, and they're . . . well, let's just say they're very particular. They're expecting the wedding of the century."

"If they're from New York City, why are they getting married in River Heights?" Bess asked.

"Bettina grew up here, and her mother still lives here," Mandy replied.

"Listen, Mandy," Nancy said slowly. "I know there's a lot to do, but I think I should spend a little time searching the house and making sure everything is okay. I have a theory that whoever locked us in the warehouse wanted us out of the way so they could set some new booby trap for tonight's wedding."

Mandy turned pale. "So you think the same person who's been doing all the other things locked you in the warehouse? And that this person might strike again tonight?"

"Yes to both questions," George said.

"Then by all means go through the house, Nancy," Mandy said immediately. "And get Rafe to help you. He should be down in his office." She turned to the cousins and added, "The three of us can manage without Nancy for a while. Bess, you can assist Daphne in the kitchen, and George . . . let's see, what can you do? There's the rest of these decorations, and there's the bride—"

While Mandy was giving instructions to George, Nancy leaned toward Bess. "While you're in the kitchen with Daphne, don't let her out of your sight, okay?" she said in a low voice. "She's our strongest suspect right now, and I want to make sure she doesn't do anything to sabotage this wedding."

"No problem," Bess replied, giving Nancy a mini salute. "I'll watch her like a hawk."

Nancy went down to the basement and knocked on Rafe's office door, which was closed. "It's me, Nancy Drew," she called out.

"Come in," Rafe replied.

Nancy entered and found Rafe hunched over his desk, scribbling furiously on a piece of paper. "How do you spell gazebo?" he murmured without looking up.

"G-A-Z-E-B-O," Nancy told him.

Rafe scribbled for another minute, then set his pen down and glanced up. "Sorry about that," he apologized. "I had to finish up my report on the damage to the gazebo. Anyway, what can I do for you? Don't tell me there's more trouble?"

"I'm not sure," Nancy said. "In any case, I wanted to search the house before the wedding started, just to make sure everything's in order."

"Actually, I was going to do that myself. But two pairs of eyes will be better than one." Rafe stood and gestured to the door. "Let's start down here and work our way up."

But after an hour of searching the house, Nancy and Rafe found nothing suspicious. "There's just the Gold Room left," Nancy said to Rafe as they lingered in the front hall. "Why don't I search that myself, since the bride and her attendants are probably getting dressed. Also, I can check out the secret passageway."

"Sounds good to me," Rafe said, nodding. "Let me know if you come across anything. I'll be in my office."

As Nancy headed up the stairs, she went over the weekend's events in her mind. The day before, there was the ghost's first appearance, then the near-theft of the wedding gifts. This morning, Nancy almost crashed her car. Then, at Kanisha and Malcolm's wedding, there was the destruction of Kanisha's dress, a second appearance by the ghost, and the gazebo incident. And finally, this afternoon, someone lured Nancy and her friends to the Excelsior Street warehouse and locked them in.

Who was behind all this? Nancy wondered. And what did he or she have planned for tonight's wedding? She was about to knock on the door to the Gold Room, when she heard, someone shrieking, *"What is happening to my dress?"*

Nancy walked apprehensively into the Gold Room and found Bettina Li, the bride, a tall, slender woman with short black hair and a tawny complexion, in hysterics. Mandy and George were with her.

Mandy was kneeling in front of Bettina, studying her strapless ivory gown. It had a full skirt and tiny beads all over the bodice.

"Is everything okay?" Nancy asked.

Mandy glanced at Nancy. "Oh, hi, Nancy. This is Bettina Li. Bettina, this is Nancy Dr—"

"I don't care if she's the First Lady of the United States!" Bettina cut in. "Can't you see that the beads are falling off this so-called dress, Mandy? I paid five thousand dollars for it. You'd think it would hold together!"

Mandy turned her attention back to the dress. "Not to worry, Bettina," she said calmly. "I have some super-strong glue in my wedding emergency kit. I'll have the beads stuck back on in no time at all."

While Mandy and Bettina dealt with the dress,

George took Nancy aside. "Did you and Rafe find anything?" she whispered.

Nancy shook her head. "No, but that doesn't mean our saboteur isn't up to something. I still want to check the secret passageway."

Bess appeared in the doorway and gestured wildly for Nancy and George to step into the hallway. Nancy and George looked at each other, then slipped out the door. George pulled it closed behind them.

"What's up?" Nancy asked Bess. "Why aren't you in the kitchen watching Daphne?"

"Well, that's the thing," Bess said, sounding agitated. "I was watching her like a hawk, as I promised, but then I turned my back on her for an itty bitty microsecond. And just like that, she was gone."

"Gone? Gone where?" George asked her.

Bess threw her hands up in the air. "That's just it. I don't know!" she cried out. "But if Daphne's the one who's been doing all the bad stuff, she may be getting ready to do something else. And it's my fault for letting her get away."

"It's okay, Bess," Nancy told her gently. "Come on, let's you and I go find her. George, you stay here with Mandy and Bettina."

"You mean Mandy and the Nightmare Bride?" George said, making a face. "Why do I always get stuck with the icky jobs?"

"You'll live," Nancy told her with a grin. She

and Bess went downstairs. Once there, they headed straight for the kitchen to see if Daphne might have returned. But she wasn't there.

The two of them combed the entire first floor with no success. However, as they passed a bay window in one of the sitting rooms, Nancy saw a woman in the backyard. She couldn't tell who it was, though; the woman was too far away.

"Maybe that's Daphne," Nancy said, pointing out the woman to Bess.

"What would she be doing outside?" Bess asked.

The two of them rushed out the front entrance and hurried across the yard. It was after seven, and the sky was a soft lavender. The air was still and cool and smelled of roses and fresh-cut grass.

The mysterious woman had long, curly hair, and was hovering near the gazebo, shrouded in shadow. Her back was to Nancy and Bess. They reached the gazebo and circled it to where the woman was standing.

That definitely looks like Daphne, Nancy thought.

Nancy cleared her throat, and the woman whirled around. Bess screamed. It was Daphne, and she was holding a knife with a long, sharp blade.

10

Plunged into Darkness

Daphne stepped back, looking startled. The blade of the knife glinted in the waning sunlight. "What are you two doing out here?" she asked.

"We could ask you the same question," Nancy replied, staring uneasily at the knife. "And what are you doing with that knife?"

Daphne glanced down. "This? I needed more fresh tarragon and sorrel for the *poulardes aux fines herbes*. I'm on my way to the herb garden to get some." Then she glanced up at Bess and gave an odd laugh. "Is that why you screamed? Because of the knife? What do I look like, an ax murderer?"

Nancy studied Daphne's face carefully. She seemed to be telling the truth, but it was hard to be sure. "Of course you don't look like an ax murderer," she said. "It's just that we're a little jumpy these days, with everything that's been going on."

"You mean the ghost and all that other stuff?" Daphne asked her.

Nancy nodded. "There's more. This morning, I almost crashed my car because someone had put red paint in the tank where the windshield cleaning fluid should have been. And this afternoon, someone called my house pretending to be Mandy and told me, Bess, and George to go to a warehouse on Excelsior Street. When we got there, the mystery caller locked us inside. We had to break a window to get out."

"You're kidding!" Daphne exclaimed. "Do you think the same person is responsible for all of these incidents?"

"It seems like it," Nancy replied, watching Daphne's reaction.

Daphne shook her head. "That's really awful," she said sympathetically. "You know, I don't understand why you guys don't just quit. I mean, who would have guessed that working for a wedding consultant could be so dangerous?"

Bess's face brightened. "That's true. We *could* just—"

"We have no intention of quitting," Nancy cut in, glancing at Bess. "There's tonight's wedding and tomorrow afternoon's, too. Besides, Mandy needs our help catching this crook, whoever he or she is."

"Well, you certainly have guts," Daphne said. "Listen, if there's anything I can do, you let me know. I'm not a detective like you, Nancy, but I've seen lots of detective shows on TV, so that's kind of close, right?" She grinned and waved her knife in the air. "I'd better get busy with those herbs. See you back in the old kitchen, Bess."

"Right," Bess said, smiling nervously at the knife.

Nancy and Bess walked back to the house, taking a shortcut through one of the perennial gardens. There were masses of yellow lilies, purple foxgloves, and fluffy pink astilbe growing in wild profusion. In the middle of it all was an ancient-looking birdbath with a cherub perched on its edge. It was made of stone, and patches of gray-green moss clung to the side of it.

As they walked, Bess turned to Nancy. "Well, what do you think of Daphne's story?"

"I don't know," Nancy said slowly. "Daphne seemed genuinely surprised when I told her about the red paint and the warehouse business. Maybe she's not behind all of this, after all." She added, "Of course, she could be a great actress. She seems to have many talents."

Nancy glanced over her shoulder, and Bess did likewise. Daphne was definitely harvesting herbs.

As the two friends continued toward the house, Nancy fell into a thoughtful silence. On the one hand, Daphne had several strikes against her. She seemed to have a motive—she bore a strong grudge against her sister—and she could have called the Drew house earlier and left the message for Nancy. And because of her former jobs, she would have had the know-how to sabotage Nancy's car and the gazebo.

On the other hand, Nancy had seen a *man* running off with Libby and Charles's wedding gifts. Plus, Daphne had not acted guilty in the least during their conversation.

Was Daphne the one? Nancy wondered. Or was it someone else altogether?

"This wedding is a total disaster," Bettina announced grimly. "First, the dress, and now, I find out that Stone's ex-girlfriend has the gall to show up here as a guest of one of his friends!"

Mandy stared helplessly at Nancy. The two of them were in the foyer outside the ballroom, helping Bettina adjust her headdress. The ceremony and dinner were over, and the black-and-white ball was in progress. The twelve-piece orchestra was playing a lively Broadway tune, and through the doorway Nancy could see dozens of couples dancing.

"I'm sorry about Stone's ex-girlfriend being here," Mandy told the bride in a soothing tone.

"But don't forget, you're the one he married, not her."

"Whatever," Bettina said sullenly. "And my parents, right? Did you hear them during cocktails? Ever since their divorce, they seem to think it's necessary to get into a loud public argument every time they see each other."

"Having divorced parents is definitely tough," Mandy said. She patted the tulle on Bettina's headdress. "Okay, you look perfect. You can go back inside and enjoy the ball now."

Bettina made a face, then disappeared into the ballroom. Mandy and Nancy lingered in the doorway. Nancy was awed by the scene before her. There were black and white silk streamers hanging from the ceiling and balconies, and everyone in the room was dressed in black and white formal wear: men in tuxedoes and women in ball gowns.

Mandy turned to Nancy. "Well, so far, so good," she said in a low voice. "We've managed to get through most of the evening without any mishaps. Maybe our ghostly saboteur gave up."

"Maybe. But we should stay on our guard, just in case," Nancy told her, scanning the crowd.

Then a familiar figure caught Nancy's eye. A young man with wavy brown hair was dancing with a petite blond woman. He was waving his arms in the air and twisting like mad, while she was dancing in a more subdued manner.

Nancy stared at the man. That's Kevin Royko, she realized, amazed.

Kevin had been at Libby and Charles's wedding and at Kanisha and Malcolm's, too. It was too much of a coincidence that he would also be a guest at *this* wedding.

"Excuse me a sec," Nancy said to Mandy. Then she entered the ballroom and went up to Bettina, who was talking to a group of people.

Nancy tapped the bride on the arm. "I'm sorry to bother you," she whispered. "But how do you happen to know that man?" She pointed Kevin out to her.

Bettina squinted. "The one who's dancing as if he's possessed by aliens?" she said disdainfully. "I've never seen him before in my life. He must be a friend of Stone's."

Nancy thanked her, then went up to Stone, who was standing alone at the punch table. Bettina's new husband was tall and angular, with thick black glasses and a long blond ponytail. "Sorry to bother you," she said to him. "I wanted to ask you about Kevin Royko."

"Kevin who?" Stone repeated, puzzled.

Nancy pointed Kevin out to him. "That man. Is he a friend of yours?"

Stone pushed his glasses up his nose and shook his head. "Definitely not. Must be a friend of Bettina's. She knows a lot of eccentric types."

Nancy thanked him and left. Maybe Kevin is

99

just a run-of-the-mill wedding crasher, she thought. Still, some instinct told her to pursue the matter a little further.

Rejoining Mandy in the foyer, Nancy asked her whether she could see the master guest list for the wedding, as well as the guest lists for the previous two weddings. "There's a man here who was at both the other weddings, too," Nancy said. "I just want to make sure he was invited to all three of them."

"No problem," Mandy said. "Follow me. I have the guest lists on my laptop."

Mandy led Nancy to a small, neatly organized office near the kitchen. "This is my workspace whenever I have an event to plan at Heights House," she explained. She sat down at the desk, got a leather briefcase out of a drawer, and pulled a portable computer out of it.

After turning it on and punching some keys, she handed it to Nancy. "Here are all three guest lists," she explained. "Just hit the menu button, and you can switch from one to another. I have to get back to the kitchen and check on the cake," she added, rising to her feet. "Let me know what you find."

Nancy thanked her and started scanning the three documents. She selected Find and punched in Kevin's name. He wasn't on any of the guest lists.

Just in case she'd misunderstood Kevin's last

name, she checked for his first name only. But the only Kevin she found was a Kevin Warshawski, and she knew there was no way she could have mistaken a long, distinctive name like that for Royko.

Bess popped her head in the door. "Mandy said you were in here," she said cheerfully. "What's going on? Catching up on your E-mail?"

"I'm trying to figure something out," Nancy said. "You remember Kevin Royko, right? Well, he's been at all three weddings this weekend. And he wasn't invited to any of them."

Bess studied her nails. "Uh-huh. So?"

"So I don't know. Still, I wonder . . ." Nancy's words trailed off, and her eyes widened. "I just remembered something else, something weird. I saw Kevin in the parking lot this morning. He was sitting in a car with a woman."

"What woman?" Bess asked.

"I ran into her in the house this morning. She looked really familiar." Nancy shut off the computer. "In any case, I want to talk to Kevin and see what his story is. Want to come with me?"

Bess nodded. "Sure."

The two of them headed for the ballroom, but when they got there, Kevin was nowhere in sight.

Nancy scanned the room, frowning. The orchestra was playing a slow, romantic song, and Bettina and Stone were swaying in the middle of the floor. A handful of couples were also dancing, and the other guests were milling around and watching. Kevin was not among them.

"He's gone," Nancy said in frustration. "I wonder where—"

"Look up there!" someone yelled. "Who is that?"

One of the guests was pointing to the balcony. The ghost—the same one Nancy had seen in the woods that morning—was standing there. It looked particularly eerie in the dim light of the ballroom.

"Nan! It's the ghost!" Bess cried out.

Almost as if the ghost had heard Bess's words, it raised one hand high in the air, then pointed a finger at her and Nancy. Bess shrieked; Nancy drew in a sharp breath. A split second later, the lights went out, and the ballroom was plunged into darkness.

11

Case Closed

Screams rang through the darkness of the ball-room. Nancy could hear people scrambling for the exits.

Bess clutched her arm. "What are we going to do, Nan?" she whispered frantically. "It's completely crazy in here, and there's a ghost on the loose!"

"We've got to calm this crowd down," Nancy said, then cupped her hands over her mouth. "Attention, everyone!" she shouted at the top of her lungs. "Please remain where you are. We've had a power failure, but we're fixing it now. The lights should be on in just a few minutes."

The announcement had the desired effect. The noise level in the room subsided somewhat, and people stopped crowding the exits.

"Good," Nancy said, satisfied. Then she turned to Bess. "Now, I think I remember seeing a large flashlight in the kitchen. Let's see if we can't find our way there."

"Whatever you say," Bess said nervously.

Nancy grabbed Bess's hand, and the two of them wove through the crowded darkness. It was a moonless night, so no light was coming through the windows. Still, some of the guests had lit matches and cigarette lighters, so Nancy and Bess were able to find their way.

They found Mandy and Daphne in the kitchen, lighting candles. Nancy could see that Mandy was close to tears.

"Our ghost struck again, just as you predicted," Mandy said shakily to Nancy. "George went down to the basement. She's going to try to get the power back on, although we hope Rafe is already working on it."

"I assume George took the flashlight, then," Nancy said. "Is there another one in here?"

Mandy shook her head. "No. Why?"

Nancy glanced around, then grabbed a few of the candles. "I'm going after that so-called ghost. I have a feeling I know where he is," she said.

Nancy handed one of the candles to Bess, then the two of them left the kitchen. Nancy started purposefully down the hall; Bess had to half run to keep up with her. "Where are we going?" she asked Nancy breathlessly.

"To the library," Nancy replied.

The hallway was spooky by candlelight. More than once, Nancy felt as though she were being followed, but it was only Bess's shadow and hers flickering on the walls. As they passed the foyer, the grim-faced portraits of Joseph and Jeanine Merrill loomed down upon them.

The portrait of Jeanine Merrill triggered something in Nancy's brain. What is it? she wondered. She reminds me of . . . And then it came to her. The woman who was sitting in the car with Kevin Royko this morning—the one Nancy had seen in the house earlier—looked just like Jeanine Merrill! The same face, the same eyes . . .

But Nancy didn't have time to dwell on this interesting new twist. She and Bess had reached the library, and Nancy went immediately to the bookshelf that led to the secret passageway. She put her ear against it; no sound came from the other side. Then, moving her fingers nimbly over the rim of the shelf, she pushed with just the right amount of pressure, and the shelf swung open silently.

Bess stared incredulously at the set of stairs that had suddenly been revealed. At the top was a landing, and beyond that the passageway curved out of sight. "We're going up *those?*" she whispered.

"*I'm* going up," Nancy said. "You stay here and

keep an eye on things. I'll call you if I need help."

Nancy took her shoes off, then started up the stairs. She moved as quietly as possible; if the ghost was indeed hiding in the secret passageway, she wanted to be able to sneak up on him. She knew there was a chance that he might see the light of her candle. Still, it was a chance she had to take; she couldn't proceed in total darkness.

Just before she reached the top of the stairs, she heard footsteps. She stopped and listened. They were fumbling, tentative steps. Someone seemed to be on the second floor, walking toward the landing.

The steps were coming closer. Nancy squeezed back against one wall of the stairs and cupped her hand over the candle flame. The steps grew closer still.

Then, suddenly, Nancy found herself staring up at the hollow, sunken eyes of the ghost. It stopped short when it saw her and whirled around to run away.

"Not so fast!" Nancy cried out, grabbing its cloak.

The cloak fell off its shoulders, and the ghost raced off in the opposite direction. Nancy dropped the cloak and ran after the ghost. Her candle blew out, and she found herself running through the complex maze in total darkness.

Robbed of sight, she tried to focus on her hearing to guide her.

Nancy could hear the ghost ahead of her and sensed that it was close enough to touch. She reached out, and her fingers grazed warm flesh. Reacting instantly, she leaped forward and tackled the ghost.

The two of them went tumbling to the floor. Nancy realized that she was in danger; for all she knew, the ghost was carrying a weapon. She struggled to find the person's arms and pin them to the floor. But the person was strong and fought back.

A golden light flickered in the passageway. Nancy glanced over her shoulder to see who was approaching. Then she heard Bess call out in a tremulous voice, "A-are you okay, Nan? I-is that the ghost?"

Distracted by Bess's presence, the ghost relaxed its struggle against Nancy for a split second. Nancy reached over and tore the skull mask from its head. At that moment Bess arrived, holding a candle high in the air.

Seeing that the so-called ghost had brown hair and freckles, Nancy knew for sure what she'd only suspected earlier. "Kevin Royko," she said slowly. "I thought that was you."

"Kevin?" Bess said disbelievingly. "*He's* our ghost?"

Kevin glared at Nancy. "That was some tackle,"

he said. "You should be playing professional football instead of detective."

Nancy let go of Kevin's wrist and eased off his back. "Don't even think about escaping," she warned him. "Now, are you ready to tell us why you've been sabotaging all these weddings?"

"What are you talking about?" Kevin rubbed his wrist gingerly, avoiding eye contact with Nancy.

"I saw you running off with Libby and Charles's wedding gifts," Nancy told him. "I didn't know it was you at the time, but now I do. You also tampered with my car, destroyed Kanisha Partridge's wedding dress, rigged the gazebo, and locked us in the warehouse this afternoon."

"You're crazy," Kevin said.

Nancy decided to take a stab in the dark. "I saw your yellow car outside the warehouse," she said smoothly. "I even got the license plate number," she added, though that wasn't true. "It's just a matter of time before the police trace it to you."

"You got the— Oh, boy." Kevin took a deep breath. "I knew I should have rented a car," he muttered.

Bingo! Nancy thought. Then she recalled the portrait of Jeanine Merrill, and another connection fell into place. "You were sitting in the parking lot with a woman this morning," she said slowly. "That was Grace Merrill Sayer, wasn't it? The granddaughter of the original owners of this house? Mrs. Sayer used to live here, but she lost the house because of back taxes, right?"

Bess gasped. "What? How do you know all this, Nancy?"

"Yeah, how *do* you know all this?" Kevin asked. He sighed and shook his head. "Oh, well. I'm going to jail no matter what, right? I might as well tell you everything."

"Good idea," Nancy said.

Kevin stared into space for a long moment. "Right, that *was* Grace Merrill Sayer you saw," he said. "She hired me to mess up all these weddings because she desperately wants her house back. She thought if word got out that Heights House was haunted, people would stop having weddings and other stuff here, and she could buy it back from the city cheaply."

"Did you mess up Nancy's car, too?" Bess asked him angrily. "You know, you could have killed her!"

"I'm really sorry about that," Kevin said. "You see, while I was snooping around the mansion I overheard a conversation you had with Mandy. Ghosts have ears, too, you know. So I figured out you were investigating. When I told Mrs. Sayer what you were doing, she freaked out. She was afraid you'd be onto us in no time. So she came up with the idea for me to go by your house in the middle of the night and put red paint in your wiper tank. She wanted to make sure you wouldn't make it to any more of the weddings." He added, "I guess I didn't think it through. It didn't occur to me that you could get into an accident."

Nancy was silent as she digested his words. Then another thought occurred to her. "Mrs. Sayer called my house this afternoon pretending to be Mandy, didn't she?" she asked Kevin. "That's why Hannah recognized her voice. The two of them went to high school together."

"They did?" Bess exclaimed. "Wow—small world!"

"Mrs. Sayer did call your house, Nancy, and I followed you guys out to the warehouse," Kevin confirmed. "Again, we were trying to keep you from making it to tonight's wedding."

Nancy nodded, then said, "How did Mrs. Sayer know that we were supposed to be here at six o'clock to help Mandy set up?"

"I overheard the two of you discussing it in the hallway this morning." Kevin pointed to Nancy and Bess.

Bess sat down on the floor next to Nancy and frowned. "There's something I don't get," she said to Kevin. "How did you manage to turn the power off while you were on the second floor?"

Kevin looked uncomfortable. "Uh, well, that was Mrs. Sayer's doing," he said after a moment.

"She's still down in the basement. In fact, I'm supposed to meet her there, although now I guess things have changed."

Nancy's eyes lit up as an idea came to her. "No, nothing's changed," she said brightly. "I want you to keep your meeting with Mrs. Sayer. But here's what I want you to do. . . ."

"Stand back," Nancy whispered to Bess and Rafe. The three of them were in the wine cellar, hiding behind a rack of dusty bottles. The power had been restored, but the only light in the wine cellar was a bare bulb that cast a dim yellow glow.

About thirty feet away, Kevin was talking to Grace Merrill Sayer, whose back was to Nancy, Bess, and Rafe.

"That was a marvelous job you did up on the balcony, Kevin," Mrs. Sayer said. "Your drama classes at college are paying off." She dug into her pocket and pulled out a bulky white envelope. "And speaking of payoffs, here's your installment for the evening."

Kevin took the envelope from her. "Thanks, Mrs. Sayer," he said. He glanced over his shoulder at Nancy, Bess, and Rafe's hiding place but quickly turned his attention back to Mrs. Sayer.

"Things are going very well, indeed," Mrs. Sayer went on eagerly. "I called the River Heights *Morning Record* earlier today and tipped them off about all the things that have been happening here this weekend. With any luck, there will be a story in Monday's paper. Heights House's reputation as a wedding site will go down in flames, and the house will be mine again."

"I think we've heard enough," Nancy whispered. She rose to her feet and stepped out from behind the wine rack. Bess and Rafe followed her.

"Not so fast, Mrs. Sayer," Nancy said.

Mrs. Sayer stared at Nancy and the others in shock. "What on earth—" she began. Then she narrowed her eyes at Kevin. "This is your doing," she muttered angrily. "You traitor! You could barely afford to pay your bills, and I came along and gave you a job. Is this how you thank me?"

"You did this to yourself, Mrs. Sayer," Nancy told her sternly. "Anyway, your game is over. It's time to deal with the authorities."

Mrs. Sayer squared her shoulders and marched up to Nancy. "That's what you think. You have no proof against me. And Kevin will never testify against me."

"Actually, that's exactly what I plan to do," Kevin shot back. "I'm sorry to do this to you, Mrs. Sayer, but I figure that if I cooperate with the police, they might go easy on me." He added, "I have to think of my future."

Mrs. Sayer gazed at him in stony silence, then at Nancy. "This is *my* house," she said after a moment. "*My* house, do you understand? I was born and raised here, and I plan to die here. You can't keep it from me!"

Before anyone knew what was happening, Mrs. Sayer reached over and picked up a dusty wine bottle from one of the racks. She whirled around, lifted the bottle high in the air, and brought it down toward Nancy's head.

12

An Ominous Note

Rafe, Bess, and Kevin rushed toward Mrs. Sayer. But Nancy managed to grab the bottle a split second before it came crashing down on her head. She pulled it loose from Mrs. Sayer's grip.

"How dare you!" Mrs. Sayer shouted. She was panting and red faced and glaring furiously at Nancy. "How dare you ruin all my plans! You don't know what it's like to lose your house—the house you grew up in, the house your family built!"

"I'm sorry about your house," Nancy said, putting the bottle back in the rack. "But that doesn't give you the right to do the things you did. You hurt a lot of people, and you nearly killed me—twice. For that you're going to have to face the music."

Mrs. Sayer opened her mouth to say something, then clamped it shut. The life was gone from her face, and she looked defeated.

Rafe stepped forward. "You'd better come with me, both of you," he ordered Mrs. Sayer and Kevin. "It's time to take a trip to the police station."

"Come on, Mrs. Sayer," Kevin said in a resigned tone. "It's the end of the road for us."

George picked up more dirty cake plates and put them on her tray. It was a few minutes after midnight, the black-and-white wedding ball was over, and the last of the guests had gone home. She, Nancy, and Bess were cleaning up in the ballroom, along with Mandy and Daphne.

"I can't believe I missed all the action tonight," George said to Nancy, who was clearing a nearby table. "While I was getting lost in the basement trying to find the circuit breaker, you were catching criminals and solving the case."

Bess, who along with Mandy and Daphne was taking down some of the decorations, turned around and put her hands on her hips. "Hey, don't forget about me!" she said. "I was catching criminals, too."

"It's definitely been quite a night," Mandy agreed. "It's been quite a *weekend*," she amended. "But thanks to you three, it's finally

115

over. No more ghosts, and no more disasters. Tomorrow's wedding should be a breeze.''

"Well, I wouldn't get too complacent about the no-more-disasters part,'' Daphne spoke up. "We have to do something about getting a new baker. And now that I think about it, I'm not too happy with our liquor distributor, either.''

Mandy stared at her in amazement. "If I didn't know better, Daph, I'd say you're actually getting into your new job,'' she said.

"I wouldn't go that far, Mandy,'' Daphne murmured, looking embarrassed. "Although I have to admit, I kind of enjoyed doing tonight's reception. The black-and-white food theme was really fun, and I got tons of compliments on my cooking.''

"You deserved them,'' Bess said, getting a dreamy look in her eyes. "That *poularde aux* whatchamacallit was awesome. And I had thirds of the black forest cake.'' She stopped and blushed. "I took a few eentsy little samples of the food during my break,'' she said sheepishly.

"No problem,'' Daphne told her, laughing. "In fact, we have tons of leftovers. Bettina and Stone asked me to donate everything to the homeless shelter.''

Mandy peered at her watch, then glanced around the ballroom. "It's so late,'' she declared. "Why don't we do a little more, and we can finish in the morning? The Fuentes-Vitale wedding isn't until one o'clock tomorrow."

"Great idea," Nancy said, yawning. "This day is catching up to me."

"Hey, what's this?" Bess asked. She bent down and picked up a folded piece of paper. "It looks as if one of the guests dropped something."

"It's probably trash," George said. "Throw it out."

Bess unfolded the piece of paper, and her eyes grew enormous. "Um, I don't think so," she said slowly. "Hey, guys, check this out."

George and the others huddled around Bess. She held up the piece of paper so everyone could see it. Written over and over again, in different handwriting styles, were the words:

YOUR WEDING IS DOOMED
STOP IT BEFORE ITS TOO LATE

"Huh?" George murmured.

"It must be one of Kevin and Mrs. Sayer's tricks," Mandy said angrily. "They probably meant for this note to get to Bettina or Stone, and it didn't happen."

"I guess either Kevin or Mrs. Sayer doesn't know how to spell," Daphne said. "There should be two *D*'s in 'weding,' and 'its' needs an apostrophe." She grinned. "I used to be a freelance copy editor, too."

117

Nancy frowned. "Why would Kevin or Mrs. Sayer write the same message over and over in different handwriting styles?" She glanced at the piece of paper again. "It's almost as though they were practicing forging someone else's hand-writing."

"Do you think we should show this to the police?" Daphne asked.

"Definitely," Nancy said, nodding. "I'll run it over there on my way home. Maybe it'll be more evidence against Kevin and Mrs. Sayer."

But when Nancy, Bess, and George swung by the River Heights Police Department half an hour later and arranged to see Kevin and Mrs. Sayer, the two of them vehemently declared they hadn't written the note.

"Give us a little credit," Kevin said. He, Mrs. Sayer, and the three girls were sitting in the visitors' room. A police officer was in the corner, watching them. "I mean, why would we leave something like this lying around on the ballroom floor?" Kevin went on. "And look at that lousy spelling! I can certainly do better than that."

Nancy gazed at Kevin thoughtfully, then fixed her eyes on Mrs. Sayer. "You didn't do this, either?" she asked her.

"Absolutely not," Mrs. Sayer said. She sat back in her chair and crossed her arms over her chest. "I'm not saying another word without having my lawyer here," she added. "I know you. You'll twist what I say and make me look guilty for things I didn't do!"

As the girls left the station, Bess turned to Nancy and asked her, "Do you believe them?"

"I guess I do," Nancy said slowly. "I mean, Kevin confessed to everything else, so why shouldn't he confess to this, too? And Mrs. Sayer seemed to be telling the truth, also." She shook her head. "But if they didn't write this note, then who did?"

"If I were you, I would just forget about it," George advised with a yawn. "It's probably somebody's idea of a joke. Or maybe a bunch of guests were sitting around a table comparing handwritings, for the fun of it."

"Maybe you're right," Nancy said. But deep down, she wasn't sure.

"That's such awful news about Grace Merrill," Hannah murmured over breakfast the next morning. "She was such a sweet girl in high school. And now, to find out that she did all those terrible things!" She shook her head.

Nancy took a sip of her coffee. "I know it," she said after a moment. "She was so desperate to get her house back, she was willing to do whatever it took, no matter how many people she hurt."

"How about her accomplice?" Carson asked her. "What's his story?"

"Kevin is a sophomore at the university and

119

one of Mrs. Sayer's neighbors," Nancy explained. "His parents stopped supporting him when he switched his major from premed to drama, and he was hard up for money. Mrs. Sayer found out and made him an offer he couldn't refuse."

"Why did she hire him to pose as a guest and attend all the weddings?" Hannah asked Nancy. "Why not just have him work behind the scenes, as they say?"

"This way Kevin had easy access to the house," Nancy replied. "I guess they didn't figure that anyone would notice his presence at all the weddings and get suspicious." She added, "He was really taking a risk getting friendly with me and with Bess, too. But he wanted to know how much I knew, and it was the only way he could find out."

Hannah dabbed at her lips with her napkin. "Well, thank goodness it's all over," she said. "I hate to think of my schoolmate in jail, but I guess that's where she belongs."

Carson turned to Nancy. "You have one more wedding this afternoon, right?"

"Right," Nancy said, nodding. "A woman named Fuentes is getting married to a man named Vitale. It's our biggest wedding of the weekend—two hundred guests, plus ten people in the wedding party."

"Good heavens!" Hannah exclaimed.

Nancy glanced at the clock on the wall. "In

fact, I should get moving," she said, rising to her feet. "I want to pick up my car at the garage. The place is closed on Sundays, but the mechanic left it out in the lot for me. Then I want to get to Heights House early. We still have lots of cleanup to do from last night."

When Nancy got to Heights House a short while later, Bess and George were already there. They were helping Mandy set up tables in the backyard for the reception.

"Good morning," Mandy called out cheerfully. "Beautiful day, isn't it?"

Nancy gazed up at the bright blue sky. "It's perfect," she declared. "What can I do?"

"You can help us with these tables, and then we'll finish cleaning the ballroom," Mandy told her.

The four of them worked diligently for the next few hours. By eleven o'clock, the tables were all in place, the house was sparkling clean, and the flowers were arranged in the chapel. In the kitchen Daphne was putting the finishing touches on an elaborate buffet lunch. The delicious smells of garlic and herbs wafted through the halls.

"The bride and her attendants should be here soon," Mandy remarked. She, Nancy, Bess, and George were in the chapel, filling tiny paper bags with birdseed for the guests to shower upon the couple. "Patti is much more, um, easy-going than last night's bride," she added in a low voice. "Of course, with a maid of honor and four bridesmaids, we'll have our work cut out for us."

A short, pretty woman with shoulder-length brown hair walked into the chapel. She was wearing jeans and a pink sweatshirt and carrying a white box in her arms.

"And there she is!" Mandy said with a smile. "Good morning, Patti! Patti, these are my assistants, Nancy, George, and Bess. Girls, this is Patti Fuentes."

"Congratulations on your big day," Bess told the bride. "How are you feeling? Are you psyched?"

Patti sat down next to Bess and the others and ran a hand through her hair. Her expression was troubled. "Actually, I'm worried sick," she said in a tense voice. "This was dropped off on my doorstep this morning." She nodded at the box in her lap.

Nancy frowned. "What's in it?" she asked Patti.

Patti took a deep breath, then opened the box. Mandy, Nancy, George, and Bess peeked in. Inside was a bride-and-groom cake ornament— or what remained of it. The heads of the figurines had been broken off.

"I don't get it," Bess murmured, puzzled. "What is this—some sick joke?"

Next to the ornament was a piece of paper. Nancy reached in, pulled it out—and gasped.

Written on it in large bold letters were the words:

YOUR WEDING IS DOOMED
STOP IT BEFORE ITS TOO LATE

13

Unexpected Danger

"The note," George said grimly to Nancy.

Patti glanced at George, then at Nancy. "What do you mean by that?" she asked sharply. "Have you seen this before?"

Nancy took a second before replying. She didn't want to tell Patti about the mishaps that had plagued the other three weddings; the bride had enough on her mind. Still, showing Patti the piece of paper from the night before might help them solve the mystery at hand.

Nancy dug into her purse and pulled out the note. "We found this on the ballroom floor last night," she said. "Do you recognize any of these handwriting variations?"

Patti scanned the piece of paper and shook her head. "N-no," she said uncertainly. "I don't understand. Does this mean that the person who sent me the box was here last night?"

"It looks that way," Nancy replied. "Listen, Patti, do you have any enemies that you know of?"

"Enemies?" Patti repeated with a nervous laugh. "I don't think so. I mean, I run a day-care center. The only people I deal with are the children and their parents."

"How about your fiancé?" George asked Patti.

"Tony runs a bookstore," Patti replied. "I can't imagine him having any enemies, either. He's the sweetest guy in the world, and all his customers love him."

Patti's eyes fell to the box in her hands. "I don't understand why someone would want to do this to me on my wedding day," she said in a trembling voice. "It's so cruel!"

"If I were you, I would put it out of my mind and concentrate on the wedding," Bess said brightly. "Why don't we go upstairs, and I'll help you get ready. Are you going to do something special with your hair? I know some tricks with a curling iron. . . ."

While Bess chattered on, Nancy turned to Mandy and George. "There's no way Kevin and Grace could have delivered the box to Patti, since they're in jail," she whispered. "That means someone else is responsible, someone who was probably a guest at last night's wedding."

"That makes sense," George said.

"I want to cross-check Patti and Tony's guest list against Bettina and Stone's," Nancy went on. "If we can find a guest who was invited to both weddings, then we may have our culprit."

"Good thinking," Mandy said, nodding eagerly. "Why don't you go work on that? The laptop's in the same place as yesterday. We'll manage without you."

Bess was still chattering away with Patti, so Nancy was able to slip out of the chapel. As she headed for Mandy's office, her mind was racing. Maybe this is an isolated incident, she thought. Maybe someone sent the broken cake ornament to Patti as a prank and has no further plans to sabotage her wedding.

Then another possibility occurred to Nancy. What if Kevin and Mrs. Sayer had an accomplice, and they planned to continue their reign of terror from jail? She made a mental note to call the police department and tell them about the broken cake ornament and note as soon as possible.

Once in the office, Nancy went right over to Mandy's desk. It was covered with files and dirty coffee cups.

Nancy cleared some space, booted up the laptop, and began punching keys. Because there was no printer available, it was difficult comparing Bettina and Stone's guest list against Patti and Tony's. But Nancy managed to find a shortcut in the computer program that enabled her to split the screen and view both documents at the same time.

After half an hour of cross-checking names, Nancy found three that were on both lists: Andrew Battista, Lars Johansson, and Kenneth Klotz. "Bingo," she said out loud. "Maybe one of them is our guy."

Nancy rummaged through Mandy's desk, found a piece of paper and a pencil, and copied the names down. As she wrote, another idea occurred to her. Bettina had complained about Stone's ex-girlfriend coming as the date of one of the guests. What if the culprit Nancy was looking for was a nameless date, and not an official guest?

"That complicates things," Nancy said to herself. "Still, these three names will give me something to work on."

When Nancy returned to the chapel, Mandy and the others weren't there. Thinking that they must be in the Gold Room, she headed upstairs.

Nancy knocked on the door and went in. Mandy, Bess, George, Patti, and her five attendants were all inside. Patti had changed into her wedding dress. Made of white satin, it had a high neck, fitted sleeves, and a full skirt that rustled elegantly when she moved. The maid of honor and the bridesmaids were all wearing pale blue dresses.

Nancy went up to Patti. "Your dress is beautiful," she said. Then she lowered her voice and added, "Could I ask you about three of your guests?"

"Um, sure," Patti said, looking surprised. "Why?"

"Remember how we thought that whoever sent you the box must have been at last night's wedding, too?" Nancy reminded her. "I cross-checked Bettina and Stone's guest list with yours and found these three people in common."

Nancy showed Patti the piece of paper with the three names on it. Patti scanned them quickly and shook her head. "There's no way Andy, Lars, or Ken could be responsible," she said. "They're all old family friends, and they would never do anything to hurt Tony or me."

"You're sure?" Nancy asked her.

"I'm positive," Patti said vehemently. Then she walked over to the dresser, picked up her purse, and pulled an envelope out of it. Inside the envelope was a group photo, which she showed to Nancy.

"I was going to give this to Andy today," Patti said. She pointed out a tall, gray-haired man with glasses, then two other men. "This is Andy, and this is Lars, and this is Ken. This picture was taken at a family picnic we had on Memorial Day, out at the lake." She glanced up at Nancy. "See, these men are like family to us. There's no way they could be guilty."

Nancy studied the picture for a moment, then nodded. "Okay, I believe you," she said. "In any case, I don't want you to worry about this for the rest of the day," she added with a smile. "You should concentrate on getting ready for your wedding." Nancy wasn't completely convinced of the three men's innocence, but she didn't want her concerns to get in the way of Patti's special day.

"Hey, Patti, what would you think if I put a lot of goop in my hair and kind of spiked it up, like this?" one of the bridesmaids called out to her.

"Don't you dare!" Patti said, laughing. Then she turned to Nancy. "Okay, I won't worry about this business anymore. You're right. I should concentrate on my wedding."

Nancy, Bess, and George stood in the hallway, watching the guests arrive. "We're looking for three older men," Nancy explained in a low voice. "One of them is tall with gray hair and glasses. The others are both shorter, with brownish gray hair and no glasses."

"So what are we supposed to do when we see them?" Bess asked her, puzzled.

"We're going to keep an eye on them during the ceremony and reception as much as we can," Nancy told her. "Patti vouched for them, but I just want to make extra sure." She nodded at a man who was walking through the front door.

"There's one of them now. I think that's Lars Johansson."

The other two men came through the door shortly thereafter and joined the stream of guests heading for the chapel. "That's all of them, then," Nancy said, satisfied.

George frowned. "You know, we have to get back to the kitchen and help out Daphne. There's no way we can keep an eye on those guys between now and the ceremony."

"I know it," Nancy said, looking troubled. "Maybe we can sneak out of the kitchen from time to time and take a peek in the chapel." She added, "Anyway, you guys go ahead. I'm going to do one final sweep of the house and make sure everything's in order."

"You're acting as though something bad's going to happen, like at the other three weddings," Bess said anxiously.

"I'm probably just overreacting," Nancy said. "Chances are, nothing will happen, and Patti and Tony will have a perfect wedding."

Bess and George headed for the kitchen, and Nancy proceeded with her survey of the house. Finding nothing unusual, she decided to check in with Rafe. She wanted to tell him about the broken cake ornament and the note. Also, she wanted to use his phone to call the police, to talk to them about this latest incident and its possible connection to Kevin and Mrs. Sayer.

She found Rafe sitting at his desk in the basement, his back to the door. "Hi, Rafe," she called out. "We've got more problems, possibly. I wanted to have a talk with you, just in case."

He didn't reply. "Rafe?" Nancy repeated, more loudly this time.

Rafe turned around in his seat. He looked haggard, and he had black circles under his eyes. He was holding the photograph of his fiancée in his hands.

Nancy glanced quickly at the photograph, then at Rafe. "Hi," she said uncertainly. "Are you okay?"

"Oh, sure, I'm fine," Rafe said with a tired-looking smile. "What's up?"

Nancy walked into the office and sat down on a folding chair next to Rafe's desk. "It's the bride," she began. "Someone delivered a box to her house this morning. It contained a bride and groom cake ornament with the heads broken off, plus a creepy note that said—"

Nancy stopped. She could see the photograph of Rafe's fiancée more clearly now, and she realized with a start who it was. She took a second, closer look to be sure, but she was right. It was none other than Patti Fuentes. Rafe had mentioned that his fiancée's name was Patricia. Patricia, Patti—they were the same woman!

Rafe followed Nancy's glance and smiled strangely. "She's beautiful, isn't she?" he mur-

131

mured. "The most beautiful woman in the world, I always told her. Today was supposed to be our wedding day, you know. Except that she left me for Tony Vitale."

Nancy forced herself to look at Rafe. "Your wedding day?" she repeated incredulously.

"That's right." Rafe's icy blue eyes gazed reverently at some point past Nancy's shoulder. "*Our* wedding day—not theirs. Of course, she's about to realize the mistake she made," he added, anger creeping into his voice. "She'll learn her lesson, and once she does, she'll come back to me."

Nancy stared at Rafe in horror. It was beginning to dawn on her that he was delusional—and probably dangerous. *He* was the one who'd sent the cake ornament and note to Patti, and *he* was the one who'd dropped the piece of paper on the ballroom floor the night before. And he seemed to have some sort of plan to stop Patti and Tony's wedding.

Nancy's mind was racing. She didn't want to tangle with Rafe alone. She was strong and trained in the martial arts, but he was powerfully built and possibly armed. Also, no one knew that she was down in the basement with him, and the wedding was due to start in a short while. If something went wrong, she would be on her own.

She took a deep breath, then fixed her eyes on Rafe, forcing herself to smile at him. "I think

Patti was crazy to choose Tony over you," she said in a sympathetic voice. "Why don't we go upstairs and talk to her now? I can help you get through to her."

"Really?" Rafe said hopefully. He sounded almost like a child.

"Really," Nancy told him. She rose from her chair and turned toward the door. *Now,* she thought, and prepared to make a run for it.

But before she could reach the door, Rafe grabbed her shoulders from behind and slammed her against the wall. Pain shot through her body, and Nancy had to bite her lip to keep from crying out.

"I'm really sorry to have to do this to you," Rafe whispered chillingly in her ear. "But I can't have anyone spoiling my plans. You understand, don't you?"

Before Nancy could reply, Rafe clamped a sweet-smelling cloth over her nose and mouth. Nancy tried to scream but couldn't. A murky darkness overtook her, and she slumped helplessly to the ground.

14

Till Death Do Us Part

Nancy woke up to the faint strains of organ music. Am I dreaming? she wondered groggily. Where am I? And then she remembered the chloroformed cloth—and Rafe.

Fueled by an adrenaline rush of fear, Nancy opened her eyes and bolted up to a sitting position. She was alone.

Glancing around, Nancy realized she was somewhere in the basement of the mansion. The walls and floors were made of concrete, and a thin shaft of sunlight was coming through a small, grimy window. The air was clammy and smelled musty.

The organ music stopped, and Nancy heard squeaking. She looked around. A rat was scurrying by her foot.

"Oh, my gosh!" Nancy cried out, and hastily drew her foot in toward her body. She stood up, and a wave of dizziness and nausea swept over her. In spite of her weakness, she began stamping her feet to frighten the rat and saw two more skittering across the floor. "I've got to get out of here," she muttered nervously.

She went over to the door. Rafe had locked it, of course. Frustrated, Nancy dug through her pockets for something with which to pick the lock. All she had was a rubber band and a safety pin.

She tried the safety pin, but it was too flimsy for the lock. She began searching the floor for something else she could use. After a while, she found a nail. "Great," she said eagerly to herself. "This should do the job!"

While she picked at the lock with the nail, one of the rats began sniffing around her ankles. Nancy backed up, took her shoe off, and threw it at the rat. The rat squeaked at her but didn't budge. Black, beady eyes glittered angrily at her.

Trying not to panic, Nancy stamped her feet again, then turned around and continued probing the lock. After a while, she heard a clicking noise. The lock was undone!

Without wasting another second, Nancy retrieved her shoe and ran out of the room, making sure to close the door behind her. Then she paused and tried to collect her thoughts. Since the organ music had stopped, she guessed that the ceremony had begun in the chapel. So where was Rafe? she wondered. And what was his plan?

Moving as quietly as possible, Nancy went to Rafe's office. The door was open. She crouched against the adjacent wall and peered in. The office was empty.

Nancy was about to head upstairs when she remembered Rafe's phone. I'd better call the police while I have a chance, she thought.

But the phone in Rafe's office had no dial tone. Frowning, Nancy pressed the button on the handset several times. The phone was dead. Nancy felt a chill go up her spine. By severing the phone lines, Rafe had cut everyone off from the outside world. The nearest house was at least two hundred yards away.

The top drawer of Rafe's desk was open a crack. Thinking that she might find a clue, she opened it all the way. Inside were at least a dozen photographs of Patti's face, as well as several dog-eared newspaper articles. Nancy picked up one of the articles. The headline read: "Man Interrupts Ex-Girlfriend's Wedding, Kills Her and Self." The headline of another article read: "Ex-Boyfriend Crashes Wedding, with Fatal Results."

Nancy gasped, then stuffed the articles back in the drawer hurriedly. I have to stop Rafe before it's too late! she thought.

She raced upstairs and headed for the kitchen, hoping to find Bess and George there. It was time to get help. Nancy was relieved to see her friends in the kitchen, cheerfully arranging hors d'oeuvres. Mandy and Daphne were inspecting potatoes.

"Nancy!" Bess exclaimed. "Where have you been? We were just about to send a search party out for you." She frowned and then added, "You look awful."

"Listen, we've got major trouble," Nancy said breathlessly. "It turns out that Rafe is Patti's old boyfriend. He plans to stop the wedding. He's a disturbed man—and very dangerous."

Mandy looked shocked. "Rafe? That nice security guard? You must be mistaken!"

"He had us all fooled, Mandy," Nancy said gravely. "I thought he was a nice guy, too, until he started ranting about how he was going to make Patti come back to him, and knocked me out with chloroform."

"Chloroform? Oh, dear, are you okay?" Mandy asked her anxiously.

"I'm fine, but we don't have any time to waste," Nancy replied. "Mandy, can you and Daphne drive to a neighbor's and call the police? The phone in Rafe's office is dead, and I assume he cut all the other phone lines, too. Bess and George—you come with me. We have to find Rafe before he hurts anyone."

"You got it," George told her, taking off her chef's apron.

Mandy and Daphne took off. George and Bess followed Nancy into the hallway. "So what's our plan?" George asked.

"I guess we should try the chapel first," Nancy replied, glancing around warily. "Keep your eyes open, though. Rafe could be anywhere."

The three of them headed down the hallway. Nancy paused at every doorway, to see if Rafe was hiding in any of the rooms. She wondered briefly if she should wait until the police arrived and let them handle the situation. But the police might not arrive for a while, and by then, it could be too late.

They finally reached the chapel. Nancy pressed her ear to the closed door; she could hear the sound of a male voice. Noiselessy, she opened the door a crack. Patti was at the altar, and a tall, slim man with curly black hair was beside her. The minister was standing before them, reciting a verse. Sunlight poured into the room through the stained-glass windows, and vases of lilacs and roses perfumed the air. The scene was deceptively peaceful, Nancy thought.

She surveyed the room, trying to find Rafe in the crowd. Because there were so many people, it was impossible to tell if he was there. She noticed an unusual number of children among the guests.

Then she remembered that Patti ran a day-care center and must have invited them to the wedding.

"Do you see him?" George whispered in her ear.

Nancy shook her head. "If only I could see the people's faces, instead of the backs of their heads!"

The minister had finished his verse and began reciting some new words. "The union between a man and a woman is the strongest bond on this earth," he said. "It is not to be entered into lightly. . . ."

"There are doors on either side of the altar," Bess told Nancy. "Maybe you could peek in without anyone noticing."

"Side doors?" Nancy repeated. Suddenly she had a bad feeling.

"If anyone here can show just cause why this man and this woman should not be joined in matrimony, let him speak now, or forever hold his peace," the minister went on.

With a sudden bang, one of the side doors burst open, and Rafe marched in, a wild look on his face. "*I* can show just cause," he announced.

"Oh, no. There he is!" Nancy gasped.

Patti threw Rafe a terrified glance and clung to Tony's arm. "Rafe!" she cried out in a trembling voice.

Tony glared at Rafe. "Who are you?" he asked. "What are you doing interrupting our wedding like this?"

"*Your* wedding?" Rafe said with a laugh. "*Your* wedding? I don't think so. Patti wants to marry *me*—don't you, Patti, dear?"

"Someone call security!" the minister said nervously. One of the children began to cry.

Rafe marched up to Patti. Tony stepped between the two of them. "You get out of here right now," Tony said, shaking his fist at Rafe.

"I'm not leaving alone," Rafe said angrily. "Patti is coming away with me right now. And if she doesn't"—he reached into his pocket and pulled out a small plastic device—"I'm going to detonate a bomb, and everyone here will die!"

15

Happily Ever After

People in the chapel began screaming. "We've got to do something!" George said frantically to Nancy.

Rafe held the device high over his head. "I've rigged a bomb to go off at the touch of a button on this remote. I'm going to press it if Patti and the rest of you don't cooperate. Do I make myself clear?"

He scanned the room with glazed eyes, then seized Patti's arm. "Please don't do this!" she cried.

Tony grabbed for Patti to get her away from Rafe. But Rafe nodded at the remote control. "You mess with me, and you're going to die, along with all these nice people here."

Tony glanced at the remote control. Then,

reluctantly, he let go of Patti and backed away. He stared helplessly at her. Rafe smiled triumphantly and put the remote control back in his pocket.

Thinking quickly, Nancy turned to Bess. "Where do those side doors lead to?" she whispered.

"They go into a little hallway in the back of the chapel," Bess said. "And that hallway kind of twists around and joins up with this hallway."

"And the closest exit is the front door," Nancy mused. "Okay, here's the plan. We're going to try to ambush Rafe—"

"An *ambush?*" Bess cut in. "Nancy, he's got a bomb. We should let the police handle it."

"But he's got Patti. If we wait for the police, it may be too late," Nancy replied tersely. "Anyway, this is what we're going to do. . . ."

After Nancy outlined the plan to her friends, they raced down the hallway. Nancy stopped when she reached a sitting room near the front entrance.

"Here," she said hastily. "You and I will hide in there, George. And Bess"—she nodded at a doorway across the hall—"can hide in there."

They assumed their positions. Nancy glanced at her watch, wondering what was taking Rafe and Patti so long. They should have been coming down the hall already, she thought anxiously.

George tapped Nancy on the arm. "What if

they went some other way?" she whispered. "Then what?"

"My guess is that he'll want to leave this place as fast as he can," Nancy whispered back. "And the front door is the closest way out." She added, "But if I'm wrong, we're in trouble. Rafe might get Patti out of the house, then blow it up anyway."

Nancy heard footsteps, the rustling of satin, then Patti's terrified voice saying, "Please don't hurt me."

"But why would I hurt you, Patti darling?" Rafe replied with a chilling laugh. "We're going to be married."

Nancy stepped back into the shadow of the doorway and motioned furiously for George and Bess to do the same. The footsteps were getting closer.

Rafe and Patti were suddenly there, walking past the hiding places. Rafe wasn't holding the remote control. It must still be in his pocket, Nancy thought.

"Now!" Nancy whispered to George.

The two of them leaped out of the doorway, jumped Rafe from behind, and grabbed each of his arms. Without missing a beat, Patti wriggled free of Rafe and moved out of the way.

"Bess!" Nancy yelled. "Search his pockets!" Rafe was strong, and Nancy didn't know how long she and George could hold him.

"Okay, okay!" Bess replied. She ran up to Rafe, dug through his pockets, and fished out the remote control. "Someone take this thing from me!" she said nervously, holding it up in the air. "I don't want to touch the wrong button!"

Nancy and George glanced at her distractedly for a split second. Rafe took the opportunity to wrench away from them. Freed, he began racing down the hall.

"He's escaping!" Patti shouted.

But Rafe hadn't counted on Nancy's speed and strength. She took off after him, diving into the air and tackling him around the waist. The two of them went down on the ground, Nancy on top. Within seconds, she had him immobilized with his arm twisted behind his back.

George, Bess, and Patti were at their sides in seconds. George knelt down beside Nancy. "Are you okay?" she asked.

"I'm fine," Nancy replied. "Where's the remote control?"

Bess held it out to her. "I still have it," she murmured unhappily. "With all this excitement, it's a miracle I didn't blow the place up."

George stared at the remote control. "That's funny," she said. "It looks like a calculator."

Nancy leaned forward and looked at the remote control. "It *is* a calculator," she said in amazement. "There never was a bomb, was there, Rafe?"

"You let go of me," Rafe cried. "Patti, make these people let go of me!"

Patti glared at him defiantly. "You're crazy, Rafe," she spat out. "You ruined my wedding and terrorized my friends and family. You're going to rot in jail for what you did!"

At that moment the front door burst open, and several police officers came rushing in. "Perfect timing," Bess declared.

"*Almost* perfect," George said. "They should have been here half an hour ago, before Patti and Tony's wedding started."

"I don't know how to thank you," Patti said gratefully to Nancy, George, and Bess. "If it weren't for you, Tony and I wouldn't have had a second chance at a wedding."

The four of them were sitting at a table on the lawn. A country band was playing a lively song, and dozens of couples were dancing on the grass. Nearby, a group of children were running around and shouting happily.

After the police had taken Rafe away, Patti had returned to the chapel and rushed tearfully into Tony's arms. Then, after a brief hiatus, the ceremony had resumed. Now the reception was in full swing, and everyone seemed to be having a good time.

Nancy picked up a small vase of lilacs from the center of the table and inhaled their sweet fragrance. "I only wish I could have stopped Rafe *before* he got to you," she said to Patti. "I didn't suspect him until I recognized your picture in his office. By then, it was too late."

Bess dunked a shrimp into some cocktail sauce on her plate. "Mmm. Almost no calories," she said. Turning to Patti, she asked, "How did you meet Rafe, anyway? He doesn't, um, seem like your type." She popped the shrimp into her mouth and chewed happily.

"He lives down the street from me," Patti replied. "He asked me out about a year and a half ago, and I said yes, mostly because I was lonely and because he seemed like a nice enough guy. But after a few dates, I lost interest. He was too intense."

"But I guess he didn't lose interest in you," George said.

Patti's expression darkened. "I guess not," she agreed. "After we stopped dating, he continued calling me. A couple of times, I even thought he was following me, but I told myself it was nothing and put the whole business out of my mind." She smiled grimly and added, "Now I know I should have taken it more seriously."

"I saw a whole bunch of photos of you in his desk," Nancy said. "Did he take them?"

Patti nodded. "He told me he was auditing a photography course at the university and asked if he could practice on me," she said. "Looking back, I'm sure that was a lie. He probably just wanted a zillion pictures of me for his private collection."

"That's a creepy thought," Bess said, and reached for another shrimp.

Tony came up to the table, bent down, and put his arm around Patti. "Hello, Mrs. Vitale," he said tenderly. "Care to dance with your new husband?"

Patti beamed at him. "I'd love to," she replied.

Tony turned to Nancy and her friends. "I can't thank you enough for what you did," he said in an emotion-filled voice.

"Oh, it was nothing," Bess told him, waving the shrimp in the air. "We do stuff like that all the time."

George stared at her cousin incredulously. "We do? In your dreams, Marvin!"

Bess popped the shrimp into her mouth and chewed.

"I'm just glad everything worked out," Nancy told Tony with a smile. "By the way, where are you going on your honeymoon?"

"Cancún, Mexico," Patti replied, excited. "I've never even been out of the country. I can't wait!"

The couple bid them goodbye and strolled away arm in arm. "I love happy endings," Bess said dreamily, watching them go. She turned to Nancy and George. "This wedding is getting me really psyched about *my* wedding. You know, I was going to do the international thing, but now I'm kind of leaning toward a Cinderella theme: a beautiful ball gown, glass slippers, a carriage, and maybe a five-course dinner made entirely of pumpkins."

"Don't you think you'd better find someone to marry you before you get too involved in planning a wedding?" George remarked dryly.

Nancy laughed, then said, "Good idea. But in the meantime, we should all get back to work, huh?"

"Work?" Bess gasped. "Haven't we done enough for one day?" Then she saw Mandy walking toward them. "Did someone say work? Let's get started!" Bess amended loudly.

Mandy plopped down on the chair Patti had vacated. "This weekend has done me in," she muttered. "Ghosts, thieves, saboteurs, and now, an obsessed ex-boyfriend. I think I need to get out of the wedding business. It's not good for my blood pressure."

"This weekend has definitely been crazy," George said.

"Little disasters, I can handle," Mandy said gamely. "Big disasters, that's another story. But now that Kevin, Mrs. Sayer, and Rafe are in jail, I suppose my worries should be over."

"Oh, definitely," Bess piped up cheerfully. "It should be smooth sailing from here on in."

Daphne came rushing up to their table. "Um, bad news," she said breathlessly. "There's been an accident."

Mandy turned white. "An accident? What sort of accident?"

Daphne averted her eyes. "I, um, kind of spilled a jar of pepper onto the wedding cake."

Nancy, George, and Bess exchanged glances. "Did someone say something about smooth sailing?" Nancy asked with a grin.

R.L. STINE'S
GHOSTS of FEAR STREET®

1 HIDE AND SHRIEK 52941-2/$3.99
2 WHO'S BEEN SLEEPING IN MY GRAVE? 52942-0/$3.99
3 THE ATTACK OF THE AQUA APES 52943-9/$3.99
4 NIGHTMARE IN 3-D 52944-7/$3.99
5 STAY AWAY FROM THE TREE HOUSE 52945-5/$3.99
6 EYE OF THE FORTUNETELLER 52946-3/$3.99
7 FRIGHT KNIGHT 52947-1/$3.99
8 THE OOZE 52948-X/$3.99
9 REVENGE OF THE SHADOW PEOPLE 52949-8/$3.99
10 THE BUGMAN LIVES! 52950-1/$3.99
11 THE BOY WHO ATE FEAR STREET 00183-3/$3.99
12 NIGHT OF THE WERECAT 00184-1/$3.99
13 HOW TO BE A VAMPIRE 00185-X/$3.99
14 BODY SWITCHERS FROM OUTER SPACE 00186-8/$3.99
15 FRIGHT CHRISTMAS 00187-6/$3.99
16 DON'T EVER GET SICK AT GRANNY'S 00188-4/$3.99
17 HOUSE OF A THOUSAND SCREAMS 00190-6/$3.99
18 CAMP FEAR GHOULS 00191-4/$3.99
19 THREE EVIL WISHES 00189-2/$3.99

Available from Minstrel® Books
Published by Pocket Books

POCKET
BOOKS

Simon & Schuster Mail Order Dept. BWB
200 Old Tappan Rd., Old Tappan, N.J. 07675

Please send me the books I have checked above. I am enclosing $_____ (please add $0.75 to cover the postage and handling for each order. Please add appropriate sales tax). Send check or money order--no cash or C.O.D.'s please. Allow up to six weeks for delivery. For purchase over $10.00 you may use VISA: card number, expiration date and customer signature must be included.

Name _____

Address _____

City _____ State/Zip _____

VISA Card # _____ Exp.Date _____

Signature _____ 1146-17

SPOOKSVILLE

- ❏ **#1 The Secret Path** 53725-3/$3.50
- ❏ **#2 The Howling Ghost** 53726-1/$3.50
- ❏ **#3 The Haunted Cave** 53727-X/$3.50
- ❏ **#4 Aliens in the Sky** 53728-8/$3.99
- ❏ **#5 The Cold People** 55064-0/$3.99
- ❏ **#6 The Witch's Revenge** 55065-9/$3.99
- ❏ **#7 The Dark Corner** 55066-7/$3.99
- ❏ **#8 The Little People** 55067-5/$3.99
- ❏ **#9 The Wishing Stone** 55068-3/$3.99
- ❏ **#10 The Wicked Cat** 55069-1/$3.99
- ❏ **#11 The Deadly Past** 55072-1/$3.99
- ❏ **#12 The Hidden Beast** 55073-X/$3.99
- ❏ **#13 The Creature in the Teacher**
  00261-9/$3.99
- ❏ **#14 The Evil House** 00262-7/$3.99
- ❏ **#15 Invasion of the No-ones**
  00263-5/$3.99

BY CHRISTOPHER PIKE

Available from Minstrel® Books
Published by Pocket Books

FOR MORE LAUGHS

TUNE IN TO

Sister Sister

ON THE
WB TELEVISION
NETWORK

(PLEASE CHECK LOCAL LISTINGS FOR DAY AND TIME)